George Peele's David and Bathsheba, and the Tragedy of Absalom: A Retelling

David Bruce

Published by David Bruce, 2022.

This is a work of fiction. Similarities to real people, places, or events are entirely coincidental.

GEORGE PEELE'S DAVID AND BATHSHEBA, AND THE TRAGEDY OF ABSALOM: A RETELLING

First edition. July 20, 2022.

Copyright © 2022 David Bruce.

ISBN: 979-8201033156

Written by David Bruce.

Table of Contents

Dedication

Dedicated to Carl Eugene Bruce and Josephine Saturday Bruce

My father, Carl Eugene Bruce, died on 24 October 2013. He used to work for Ohio Power, and at one time, his job was to shut off the electricity of people who had not paid their bills. He sometimes would find a home with an impoverished mother and some children. Instead of shutting off their electricity, he would tell the mother that she needed to pay her bill or soon her electricity would be shut off. He would write on a form that no one was home when he stopped by because if no one was home he did not have to shut off their electricity.

The best good deed that anyone ever did for my father occurred after a storm that knocked down many power lines. He and other linemen worked long hours and got wet and cold. Their feet were freezing because water got into their boots and soaked their socks. Fortunately, a kind woman gave my father and the other linemen dry socks to wear.

My mother, Josephine Saturday Bruce, died on 14 June 2003. She used to work at a store that sold clothing. One day, an impoverished mother with a baby clothed in rags walked into the store and started shoplifting in an interesting way: The mother took the rags off her baby and dressed the infant in new clothing. My mother knew that this mother could not afford to buy the clothing, but she helped the mother dress her baby and then she watched as the mother walked out of the store without paying.

My mother and my father both died at 7:40 p.m.

Cover Photograph for George Peele's *David and Bathsheba, and the Tragedy of Absalom*: A Retelling:

https://pixabay.com/photos/girl-woman-erotica-topless-breast-4577854/

https://www.instagram.com/victoriaborodinova/?hl=en
https://www.facebook.com/victoria.borodinova
https://pixabay.com/users/victoria_borodinova-6314823/

Educate Yourself
Read Like A Wolf Eats
Be Excellent to Each Other
Books Then, Books Now, Books Forever

****

In this retelling, as in all my retellings, I have tried to make the work of literature accessible to modern readers who may lack some of the knowledge about mythology, religion, and history that the literary work's contemporary audience had.

Do you know a language other than English? If you do, I give you permission to translate this book, copyright your translation, publish or self-publish it, and keep all the royalties for yourself. (Do give me credit, of course, for the original retelling.)

I would like to see my retellings of classic literature used in schools, so I give permission to the country of Finland (and all other countries) to give copies of this book to all students forever. I also give permission to the state of Texas (and all other states) to give copies of this book to all students forever. I also give permission to all teachers to give copies of this book to all students forever.

Teachers need not actually teach my retellings. Teachers are welcome to give students copies of my books as background material. For example, if they are teaching Homer's *Iliad* and *Odyssey*, teachers are welcome to give students copies of my *Virgil's Aeneid: A Retelling in Prose* and tell students, "Here's another ancient epic you may want to read in your spare time."

CAST OF CHARACTERS

David and his Family:

David, King of Israel and Judah.

Cusay, a lord, and follower of David.

Amnon, son of David by David's first wife: Ahinoam. He is David's oldest son.

Jethray, Servant to Amnon.

Chileab, son of David by Abigail.

Absalom, son of David by Maacah. George Peele called him Absalon.

Thamar, daughter of David by Maacah.

Adonia, son of David by Haggith.

Solomon, son of David by Bathsheba. George Peele called him Salomon.

Joab, captain of the army to David, and nephew of David and son of his sister Zeruia.

Abisai, nephew of David and son of his sister Zeruia.

Amasa, nephew of David and son of his sister Abigail; also captain of the army to Absalom.

Jonadab, nephew of David and son of his brother Shimeah; also friend to Amnon.

Other Characters:

Uriah the Hittite, a warrior in David's army. George Peele called him Urias the Hethite.

Bathsheba, wife of Uriah. George Peele called her Bethsabe.

Maid to Bathsheba.

Nathan, a prophet.

Sadoc, high priest.

Ahimaas, his son.

Abiathar, a priest.

Jonathan, his son.

Achitophel, chief counselor to Absalom.

Ithay, a captain from Gath.

Semei, who hates David.

Hanon, King of Ammon.

Machaas, King of Gath.

Woman of Thecoa.

Messenger, Soldiers, Shepherds, and Attendants.

Concubines to David.

Chorus.

NOTES:

I have used the names we know the characters by instead of George Peele's names.

- His Bethsabe is our Bathsheba.
- His Absalon is our Absalom.
- His Urias the Hethite is our Uriah the Hittite.
- His Salomon is our Solomon.

Zion is the city of David: the Jerusalem of ancient times.

Often, George Peele will use Jerusalem when he means Israel; thus, in one sentence he will refer first to Jerusalem (Israel) and then to Zion (Jerusalem).

George Peele's play often uses the name "Jove" for God. Jove is, of course, Jupiter, a pagan god. This use of "Jove" for God is common among Elizabethan playwrights.

In Elizabethan culture, a man of higher rank would use words such as "thee," "thy," "thine," and "thou" to refer to a servant. However, two close friends or a husband and wife could properly use "thee," "thy," "thine," and "thou" to refer to each other.

The Elizabethans believed that the mixture of four humors in the body determined one's temperament. One humor could be predominant. The four humors are blood, yellow bile, black bile, and phlegm. If blood is predominant, then the person is sanguine (optimistic). If yellow bile is predominant, then the person is choleric (bad-tempered). If black bile is predominant, then the person is melancholic (sad). If phlegm is predominant, then the person is phlegmatic (calm).

RECOMMENDED EDITION

Here is an excellent annotated edition of the play, which can be downloaded free:

Peele, George. *David and Bethsabe*. Annotated Edition. ElizabethanDrama.org, 2019. Web.

<https://tinyurl.com/yetjbpro>

The man behind ElizabethanDrama.org is Peter Lukacs.

The ElizabethanDrama.org edition of the play quotes from the 1568 Bishop's Bible, which was the main Bible that George Peele used in writing this play. The ElizabethanDrama.org edition modernizes the spelling of that Bible, and my retelling of George Peele's play uses some of those modernized-spelling quotations.

Many Elizabethan plays are based on mythology, but this is the only extant play based solely on the Bible (and the playwright's imagination). The ElizabethanDrama.org edition identifies the Biblical source, when relevant, of each scene:

Bible Verses Described by the Prologue: None.

Bible Verses Depicted in Scene I: 2 Samuel 11:1-6.

Bible Verses Depicted in Scene II: 2 Samuel 12:26-28.

Bible Verses Depicted in Scene III: 2 Samuel 13:1-7.

Bible Verses Depicted in Scene IV: 2 Samuel 13:15-20.

Bible Verses Depicted in Scene V: lines 1-64: 2 Samuel 13:21, 23-27; after that, 2 Samuel 11:7-15.

Bible Verses Described by the Chorus I: 2 Samuel 11:16-17, 26-27; and 2 Samuel 12:14.

Bible Verses Depicted in Scene VI: 2 Samuel 12:15.

Bible Verses Depicted in Scene VII: 2 Samuel 12:1-24.

Bible Verses Depicted in Scene VIII: 2 Samuel 13:27-29.

Bible Verses Depicted in Scene IX: all the indicated verses are from 2 Samuel: (1) lines 1-86, 12:29-31; (2) lines 87-140, 13:30-33; (3) lines 142-218, 14:1-23; (4) lines 220-225, 14:25-26; (5) lines 227-247, 14:33; and (6) lines 249-266, 15:1-6.

Bible Verses Depicted in Scene X: 2 Samuel 15:17-37.

Bible Verses Depicted in Scene XI: 2 Samuel 16:15-17:21.

Bible Verses Depicted in Scene XII: all the indicated verses are from 2 Samuel: (1) lines 1-99, 16:5-13; (2) lines 101-132, 17:21-22; and (3) 134-174, 18:1-5.

Bible Verses Depicted in Scene XIII: 2 Samuel 17:23.

Bible Verses Depicted in Scene XIV: None.

Bible Verses Depicted in Scene XV: 2 Samuel 18:6-17.

Bible Verses Described by the Chorus II: None.

Bible Verses Depicted in Scene XVI: None.

Bible Verses Depicted in Scene XVII: there are no verses in the Bible corresponding to lines 1-151; lines 153 to the end of the scene match up with 2 Samuel 18:24-19:8.

PROLOGUE

An actor sings the Prologue. In addition to praising King David of Israel, who both composed many songs of praise to God and achieved many military victories for his country, the actor asks a Muse for help in telling King David's story.

"Of Israel's sweetest singer now I sing,

"His holy style and happy victories;

"Whose Muse was dipped in that inspiring dew

"Archangels distilled from the breath of Jove,

"Adorning her temples with the glorious flowers

"Heavens rained on the tops of Zion and Mount Sinai.

"Upon the bosom of his ivory lute

"The cherubim and angels laid their breasts;

"And, when his consecrated — sacred — fingers struck

"The golden wires of his ravishing harp,

"He gave alarum to [alerted] the Host [Army] of Heaven,

"The angels who, winged with lightning, broke through the clouds, and cast

"Their crystal armor at his conquering feet.

"Of this sweet poet, Jove's musician,

"And of his beauteous son Absalom, I strive to sing.

"Help, divine Adonai [God], to conduct

"Upon the wings of my well-tempered and pleasant verse

"The hearers' minds above the towers of Heaven,

"And guide them so in this thrice-lofty flight

"That their mounting feathers are not scorched by the fire

"That none can temper but Thy holy hand.

"To Thee for succor flies my feeble Muse,

"And at Thy feet her iron pen does use."

In this case, the Muse is too weak to tell David's story and so the playwright must ask Adonai — another name for God — for help.

The Muse's iron pen is a chisel. Words written in rock with a chisel have permanence.

CHAPTER 1

On the roof of the Royal Palace in Jerusalem, King David sat and watched Bathsheba below bathing over a spring. Bathsheba, the wife of Uriah, a soldier in King David's army, was unaware that King David was watching her bathe. She sang as she bathed herself:

"Hot sun, cool fire, tempered with sweet air,

"Black shade, fair nurse, shadow [screen] my white hair:

"Shine, sun; burn, fire; breathe, air, and ease me;

"Black shade, fair nurse; shroud me, and please me:

"Shadow, my sweet nurse, keep me from burning,

"Make not my glad cause a cause of mourning."

Bathsheba was beautiful, and she was blonde. She wanted her skin — a reason for her happiness — to remain fair and not burn in the strong sunlight.

"Let not my beauty's fire

"Inflame unstaid [immoderate] desire,

"Nor pierce [penetrate] any bright eye

"That wanders lightly."

The word "lightly" can mean 1) unthinkingly, or 2) wantonly.

Bathsheba then said, "Come, gentle Zephyr, you west wind, adorned with those perfumes that formerly in Eden sweetened Adam's love — Eve — and stroke my bosom with thy silken-soft fan.

"This shade, sun-proof, is yet no proof against thee. Thy body, smoother than this waveless spring, and purer than the substance of the same, can creep through that which his lances cannot pierce. Thou, Zephyr, and thy sister, soft and sacred Air, goddess of life, and governess of health, keep every fountain fresh and arbor sweet. No brazen gate can repulse her passage, nor can bushy thicket bar thy subtle, fine, delicate breath.

"So then deck thyself with thy loose delightsome — delightful — robes, and on thy wings bring delicate perfumes to play the wantons with us through the leaves."

King David said to himself, "What tunes, what words, what looks, what wonders pierce my soul, incensed and inflamed with a sudden fire? What tree, what shade, what spring, what paradise, enjoys the beauty of so fair a dame?

"Fair Eve, placed in a garden of perfect happiness, lending her praise-notes to the liberal heavens and praising in song the generous heavens, singing with the accents of archangels' tunes, did not bring more pleasure to her husband Adam's thoughts than this fair woman's words and notes bring to my thoughts.

"May that sweet plain that bears her pleasant weight be always enameled with flowers of many colors.

"May that precious spring bear sand of purest gold, and, for the pebbles, let the silver streams that pierce the earth's bowels to maintain the source, play upon rubies, sapphires, and green-colored gems.

"Let the waters be embraced with and surrounded by golden curls of moss that sleep with the sound the waters make out of joy at feeding the spring with their flow.

"Let all the grass that beautifies her shady bower bear the Biblical food called manna every morning instead of dew, and let the dew be sweeter far than the dew that hangs, like chains of pearl, on high Hermon Hill, and sweeter far than the balm that trickled from old Aaron's beard."

Psalms 133:3 states, "*It is also like unto the dew of Hermon, which falleth down the hill of Zion*" (1568 Bishop's Bible).

Psalms 133:2 states, "*It is like unto a precious ointment poured upon the head, which runneth down upon the beard, even upon Aaron's beard, which also runneth down the skirts of his garments*" (1568 Bishop's Bible).

Aaron was the brother of Moses, and he was a high priest.

King David then called for a servant: "Cusay, come up, and serve thy lord the king."

Cusay arrived and asked, "What service does my lord the king command?"

King David replied, "Look, Cusay, see the flower of Israel, the fairest daughter who obeys the king in all the land the Lord subdued to me."

He was referring to Bathsheba, his subject.

He continued, "She is fairer than Isaac's lover at the well, brighter than the inside-bark of new-hewn cedar, sweeter than flames of fine-perfumed myrrh, and comelier — more beautiful — than the silver clouds that dance on Zephyr's wings before the King of Heaven."

Genesis 24 tells the story of how Isaac, the son of Abraham, married. Abraham wanted Isaac to marry a woman from Mesopotamia, so Abraham sent his oldest servant to find a wife for Isaac. The servant arrived at a Mesopotamian well and prayed. Rebecca came to the well, drew water, and gave the servant water to drink. Rebecca became Isaac's wife.

Cusay asked, "Isn't she Bathsheba, the wife of the Hittite Uriah, who is now at the siege of Rabbah under the command of Joab?"

Rabbah was about 40 miles northeast of Jerusalem. It was the capital city of Ammon.

King David ordered, "Go and find out, and bring her quickly to the king: me. Tell her that her graces have found grace with him."

"I will, my lord," Cusay said.

He exited.

King David said to himself, "Bright Bathsheba shall wash, in David's bower, in water mixed with purest almond-flower, and bathe her beauty in the milk of young goats.

"Bright Bathsheba gives earth to my desires. She gives verdure — lush green vegetation — to earth, and to that verdure she gives flowers.

To flowers she gives sweet odors, and to odors she gives wings that carry pleasures to the hearts of kings."

Cusay appeared at the spring below the palace, startling and frightening Bathsheba.

Cusay said, "Fair Bathsheba, the King of Israel from forth his princely tower has seen thee bathe, and thy sweet graces have found grace with him. Come, then, and kneel to him where he stands; the king is gracious and has liberal and generous hands."

She replied, "Ah, who and what is Bathsheba to please the king? And who and what is David, that he should desire, for fickle beauty's sake, the wife of his servant?"

Beauty is fickle: It doesn't last. It moves on to someone else.

Uriah, a soldier in King David's army, was the servant whose wife she was.

Bathsheba knew immediately that King David wanted to sleep with her.

Cusay replied, "Thou, fair dame, know that David is wise and just, elected to the heart of Israel's God. So then don't expostulate with him about any action that contents his soul."

Bathsheba replied, "My lord the king, elect to God's own heart, should not inflame his gracious jealousy — his thoughts are chaste. I hate incontinence."

The word "his" could refer to Bathsheba's husband, to God, or to King David — or to all three.

"Jealousy" is a strong emotion. Bathsheba's husband would be jealous if King David were to sleep with her. God is a jealous god because he feels strong emotion when people follow false idols and commit sin. King David ought to have the same kind of gracious jealousy that a husband or the one true God ought to have. Instead, the strong emotion that King David was feeling was sexual desire. He was jealous of Bathsheba's husband.

Cusay said, "Woman, thou wrong the king, and doubt the honor of him whose truth maintains the crown of Israel. You are making him wait who ordered me to bring thee to him immediately."

"The king's poor handmaid will obey my lord," Bathsheba said.

"Then come, and do thy duty to his grace," Cusay said. "Do what seems favorable in his sight."

Bathsheba and Cusay went into the palace.

King David said, "Now comes my lover trippingly like the roe deer, and she brings my longings tangled in her hair. As a place to enjoy her love, I'll build a kingly bower, seated within the sound of a hundred streams, which, for their homage to her greatest joys, shall, just like the serpents fold into the serpents' nests in oblique turnings, wind their nimble waves about the circles of her elaborate walks; and with their murmur summon easeful Sleep to lay his golden scepter on her brows."

Hearing Cusay and Bathsheba coming, King David ordered his attendants, "Open the doors, and welcome my love. Open, I say, and, as you open, sing, 'Welcome, fair Bathsheba, King David's darling.'"

Cusay and Bathsheba entered.

King David and the attendants sang to Bathsheba, "Welcome, fair Bathsheba, King David's darling."

He then said, "Thy bones' fair covering was previously revealed to be fair and beautiful, and all my eyes were pierced with all thy beauties.

"Heaven's bright eye — the sun — burns most when highest it climbs the curved zodiac with its fiery sphere, and shines furthest from this earthly globe. Therefore, since thy beauty scorched my conquered soul, I called thee nearer for my nearer cure."

A temporary cure for sexual passion is an orgasm.

Bathsheba replied, "Too near, my lord, was your unprotected heart when furthest off it pierced my luckless beauty, and I wish that this dreary day had turned to night, or that some pitch-dark cloud had cloaked the sun, before their lights — the light of the day and the light of the sun — had caused my lord to see his name and my chastity disgraced!"

So far, Bathsheba had been a chaste wife: She was loyal to her husband and had not slept with anyone else. King David, however, was a powerful man who intended to make her unchaste.

King David replied, "My love, if want of love has left thy soul a sharper sense of honor than that possessed by thy king — for love leads kings sometimes from their thrones, making them behave inappropriately — as formerly my heart was hurt, displeasing thee, so come and taste thy ease with easing me."

King David knew what he wanted: sex with Bathsheba. Her husband was a soldier who was away on a military campaign, and so she lacked sex, which according to King David's view, meant that she wanted sex. He had displeased her, which he said hurt his heart, and now he wanted her to ease his hurt by sleeping with him. If she did, she would "taste her ease" — that is, she would enjoy herself.

To King David, this may have made some kind of sense — he was thinking with his penis — but it did not make sense to Bathsheba.

She replied, "One medicine cannot heal our different harms, for the one medicine would rather make us both fester at the bone. So then let the king be cunning in his cure, lest by his flattering and misleading both of us, both of us perish in his hand."

King David's harm was that he wanted to have sex with Bathsheba; Bathsheba's harm was that she was being pressured to have sex with King David, a man with whom she did not want to have sex.

The medicine that King David was advocating was sex, but that would "cure" only one of their harms.

The harms were also sins: King David wanted to commit adultery, and he wanted Bathsheba to commit adultery. These actions would make them metaphorically fester at the bone.

In a Christian world-view, sin can cause one to perish. If King David were to commit adultery with Bathsheba, both of them could perish.

King David said, "Leave it to me, my dearest Bathsheba, whose skill is conversant in deeper cures."

The best cure is prevention: Don't commit adultery and bring that harm on yourself. This is not what King David had in mind.

King David ordered, "Cusay, hasten to my servant Joab and command him to send Uriah home with all the speed that can possibly be used."

"Cusay will fly about the king's desire," Cusay replied, exiting.

CHAPTER 2

— Scene 2 —

Joab, Abisai, and Uriah stood before the walls of the city of Rabbah, the capital city of Ammon. Others, including a drummer and an ensign who carried the army's banner, were present. Joab, the commanding officer, was King David's nephew. Abisai was Joab's brother, and so he was another of King David's nephews. Uriah was Bathsheba's husband. Both Abisai and Uriah were elite soldiers.

Nahas, the King of Ammon, had helped David before David became King of Israel. When King Nahas died, King David sent some ambassadors to the late king's son, Hanon, in Rabbah. King Hanon, however, was convinced that the ambassadors were spies, so he cut off half of each man's clothing and half of each man's beard and sent them thus disgraced back to King David.

King David sent Joab to lead the Israelite army against Ammon. The Israelites defeated the Ammonite army and their Syrian mercenaries. The following spring, the Israelite army, again led by Joab, returned and again defeated the Ammonite army. They then besieged Rabbah, the capital city of Ammon.

The above events are recounted in 2 Samuel 10.

Joab said, "Have courage, you mighty men of Israel, and discharge your fatal instruments of war upon the bosoms of proud Ammon's sons, who have insulted your king's ambassadors by cutting half of each man's beard and half of each man's garments off, to spite Israel and Israel's daughters' sons!

"You fight the holy battles of Jehovah, King David's God, and ours, and Jacob's God, Who guides your weapons to their conquering strokes, orders your footsteps, and directs your thoughts to stratagems that harbor victory.

"He casts his sacred eyesight from on high, and sees your foes run seeking their deaths."

The enemy think that by running away they are seeking to save their lives, but God, Who is omniscient, knows that they will die. Or the enemy run to fight David's soldiers, but God, Who is omniscient, knows that they will die.

Joab continued, "God laughs their labors and their hopes to save their lives to scorn, while between your bodies and their blunted, edgeless swords, he puts armor of his honor's proven and tested value, and he makes their weapons wound the sense-less winds."

The winds are without senses: They are unable to see, hear, smell, taste, or feel.

Abisai, an elite soldier, said, "Before this city of Rabbah we will lie, and shoot forth shafts as thick and dangerous as was the hail that Moses mixed with fire, and threw with fury round about the fields, devouring Pharaoh's friends and Egypt's fruits."

The seventh plague of Egypt was a thunderstorm of hail and fire (lightning).

Uriah, another elite soldier, said, "First, mighty captains, Joab and Abisai, let us assault and scale this kingly tower, where all their conduits and their fountains are. Then we may easily take the city, too."

The city of Rabbah had two parts: an upper part and a lower part. The lower part had a tower and contained the city's water supply. Once the upper part ran out of water, it would fall.

Joab said, "Well has Uriah counseled our military efforts; and as he recommended us, we will assault the tower. Let Hanon now, the king of Ammon's sons, repulse our conquering passage if he dare."

King Hanon of Ammon appeared upon the walls of Rabbah with Machaas, who was the King of Gath. Some soldiers and attendants also appeared with them.

King Hanon said, "What would the shepherd's dogs of Israel snatch from the mighty issue of King Ammon: the valiant Ammonites and the proud Syrians?"

His issue was his citizens, who were metaphorically his children.

The Syrians were allies of Ammon.

He continued, "Your recent successive victories cannot make us yield, and they cannot make our courage quail. If you dare attempt to scale this tower, our angry swords shall smite you to the ground, and avenge our losses on your hateful lives."

Joab said, "Hanon, thy father Nahas gave relief to holy David in his luckless exile, lived his fixed period of life, and died in peace. But thou, instead of reaping his reward, have trodden it under foot, and scorned our king; therefore, thy days shall end with violence, and thy vital blood shall cleave to our swords."

King Hanon's ally, King Machaas of Gath, a Philistine city located approximately 30 miles southwest of Jerusalem, said, "Go away from here, thou who bear poor Israel's shepherd's hook, the proud lieutenant of that base-born king, and keep within the compass of his sheepfold."

David had been a shepherd before becoming King of Israel.

King Machaas of Gath continued, "For, if you seek to feed on Ammon's fruits, and stray into the Syrians' fruitful meadows, the mastiffs of our land shall torment you, and pull the windpipes from your greedy throats."

"Who can endure these pagans' blasphemies?" Abisai said.

"My soul feels discontent at this disparagement," Uriah said.

Joab said, "You valiant men of David's army, attack and beat these insulting cowards from their doors."

The Israelites attacked and seized the tower and the lower part of the city.

Joab said, "Thus have we won the tower, which we will keep, in spite of the sons of Ammon and of Syria."

Cusay arrived outside the city and asked, "Where is Lord Joab, leader of the army?"

Joab said, "Here is Lord Joab, leader of the army. Cusay, come up, for we have won the stronghold."

"In a happy hour, then, has Cusay come," Cusay replied.

Cusay went up to Joab and the others in the conquered part of the city.

"What news, then, does Lord Cusay bring from the king?" Joab asked.

"His majesty commands thee immediately to send home Uriah from the wars, because of some service Uriah should do," Cusay said.

Uriah said, "I hope that no anger has seized the king and made him suspect that I am disloyal."

"No, it has not," Cusay said. "Rather, he wants to show you favor on account of your loyalty to him."

"Here, take him with thee, then, and go in peace," Joab said. "And tell my lord the king that I have fought against the city of Rabbah with success, and scaled where the royal palace is, as well as the conduit-heads and all their sweetest springs. King David can come in person to these walls, with all the soldiers he can bring with him, and capture the city as his own exploit, lest I surprise it, and the people give the glory of the conquest to my name."

Joab was generously telling Cusay that King David could come and capture the top part of Rabbah, thereby taking the credit for capturing the city.

"We will give him your message, Lord Joab," Cusay said, "and may great Israel's God bless in thy hands the battles of our king!"

"Farewell, Uriah," Joab said. "Hurry to see the king."

Uriah replied, "As surely as Joab breathes as a victor here, Uriah will hasten to see King David and then return."

Cusay and Uriah exited.

"Let us descend from the walls we are on, and open the palace's gate, taking our soldiers in to keep the stronghold," Abisai said.

"Let us, Abisai," Joab said.

He added, "And, you sons of Judah, be valiant, and maintain your victory."

CHAPTER 3

Amnon, Jonadab, and Jethray stood together outside Amnon's house in Jerusalem. Amnon's page — a young servant — was also present.

Amnon was David's oldest son: the son of David by Ahinoam. Jonadab was the nephew of David and son of his brother Shimeah; he was a friend as well as a first cousin to Amnon. Jethray was one of Amnon's servants.

Jonadab said to Amnon, "You wear upon your truly triumphant arm the power of Israel as a royal favor, and you hold upon the tables of your hands banquets of honor and all thought's contentment."

Amnon was privileged. As a son of King David, he had much power and wealth. All his power and wealth was like a feast. He seemed to have everything needed to make him happy, yet he looked ill.

Jonadab then asked Amnon, "What means my lord, the king's beloved son, to allow pale and grim abstinence to sit and feed upon his fainting cheeks, and suck away the blood that cheers his looks?"

Despite having a feast of power and wealth, Amnon looked as if he were wasting away.

Amnon replied, "Ah, Jonadab, it is my half-sister Thamar's looks, on whose sweet beauty I bestow my blood, that make me look so amorously lean. Her beauty having seized upon my heart, so entirely consecrated — dedicated — to her contentment, sets now such a guard about his vital blood, and views the passage with such piercing eyes that no blood can escape to cheer my pining, wasting-away cheeks, but all is thought too little for her love."

According to Amnon, he appeared bloodless because his lovesickness for his half-sister kept his blood from flowing freely.

Jonadab said, "Then from her heart thy looks shall be relieved, and thou shall enjoy her as thy soul desires."

To "enjoy" a woman meant to have sex with her.

Amnon asked, "How can that be, my sweet friend Jonadab, since Thamar is a virgin and my half-sister?"

Thamar and Amnon shared the same father: King David.

Quickly coming up with a plan, Jonadab answered, "Do as I advise thee. Lie down upon thy bed and pretend that thou are fever-sick and ill at ease. When the king shall come to visit thee, request that thy half-sister Thamar may be sent to prepare some delicacies for thy malady. Then when thou have her solely with thyself, *enforce some favor to thy manly love.*"

Jonadab used a euphemism to say, "Rape her."

He looked up and said, "See where she is coming here. Ask her to go inside with thee."

Thamar entered the scene and asked, "What is ailing Amnon, causing such sickly looks to lessen the attractiveness of his lovely face?"

Amnon replied, "Sweet Thamar, I am sick, and I wish for some wholesome delicacies prepared with the skill of thy dainty hands."

"The king has already commanded me to do that," Thamar said. "So then come and rest thyself, while I prepare for you some delicacies that will ease thy impaired soul."

"I go with thee, sweet half-sister," Amnon said. "Looking at thee eases my pain."

Thamar, Amnon, Jethray, and the page exited.

Staying behind, Jonadab said to himself, "Why should a prince, whose power may command others to serve him, obey the rebel passions of his love when they contend just against his conscience and may be governed or suppressed by will?"

According to Jonadab, Amnon ought to be able to control his passion for his half-sister. Amnon had the power to control other people, so why shouldn't he be able to control himself?

Jonadab continued, "Now, Amnon, loose those loving knots of blood that sucked the courage from thy kingly heart and give it passage to thy withered cheeks."

By raping his half-sister, Amnon would be able to satisfy his lustful passion and regain the bloom in his cheeks.

Jonadab continued, "Now, Thamar, ripened are the holy fruits that grew on the plants of thy virginity, and rotten is thy name in Israel."

By losing her virginity without first being married, Thamar would lose her good reputation.

Jonadab continued, "Poor Thamar, little did thy lovely hands predict an action of such violence as to contend with Amnon's lusty arms muscled with the vigor of his kind-less love."

This sort of "love" was without kindness, and it was not the sort of love that a man ought to feel toward kin such as a half-sister.

Jonadab continued, "Fair Thamar, now dishonor hunts thy foot, and follows thee through every concealing shade, revealing thy shame and nakedness, even from the valleys of the land called Jehosaphat up to the lofty mountains of Lebanon, where cedars, stirred with the anger of the winds, sounding in storms the tale of thy disgrace, tremble with fury, and with murmur shake the earth with their feet and shake the heavens with their heads, beating the clouds into their swiftest movement, to bear this wonder round about the world."

Now that Thamar had lost her virginity without first being married, dishonor would follow at her footsteps wherever she went, and even the wind would spread the news of her dishonor throughout the world.

CHAPTER 4

Amnon thrust Thamar outside his house. Jethray, his servant, was present.

Ammon said, "Go away from my bed, you whose sight offends my soul as does the vomit of bears!"

His half-sister, Thamar, said, "Unkind, unprincely, and unmanly Amnon, to rape, and then refuse thy half-sister's love, adding to the fright of thy offence the baneful torment of my well-publicized shame! Oh, don't do this dishonor to thy love, nor clog thy soul with such increasing sin! This second evil far exceeds the first."

By thrusting Thamar out of his house, Amnon was exposing her to the contempt and hatred of other people, thereby shaming her. To Thamar, this was far worse than being raped.

Amnon ordered his servant, "Jethray, come thrust this woman away from my sight, and bolt the door against her if she resists and tries to get back inside."

He exited.

Jethray said to Thamar, "Go, madam, go. Go away, you must leave. My lord has done and finished with you. I beg you to depart."

He shut her out of doors and exited.

Thamar said to herself, "Whither, alas, ah, whither shall I flee, with my arms wrapped around myself and with my completely dumbfounded soul?

"Cast away as Eve was from that glorious soil — that glorious garden where all delights sat fluttering, winged with thoughts, ready to nestle in her naked breasts — to bare and barren valleys made waste with floods, to deserted woods, and lightning-scorched hills, sites with death, with shame, with Hell, with horror.

"There will I wander from my father's face. There Absalom, my brother Absalom, sweet Absalom, shall hear his sister mourn. There will I lure with my windy sighs night-ravens and owls to rend and tear my bloody side, which with a rusty weapon I will wound, and make for them a passage to my panting heart.

"Why do thou talk, wretch, and leave the deed undone?

"Rend and tear thy hair and garments, as thy heart is rent and torn with the inward fury of a thousand griefs, and scatter them by these unhallowed and unholy doors, to represent Amnon's wresting, tearing cruelty and the tragic spoil of Thamar's chastity."

Her full brother, Absalom, appeared on the scene. He had heard his sister crying out.

Absalom asked, "What causes Thamar to exclaim so much?"

She replied, "The cause that Thamar is ashamed to disclose."

"Tell me," Absalom said. "I thy brother will revenge that cause."

"Amnon, our father's son, has raped me, and he thrusts me away from him as the scorn of Israel," Thamar said.

"Has Amnon raped thee?" Absalom said. "By David's hand, and by the covenant God has made with him, I swear that Amnon shall bear his violence to Hell. Amnon is a traitor to Heaven, a traitor to David's throne, and a traitor to Absalom and Israel!

"This evil deed has Jacob's ruler — God — seen from Heaven, and through a cloud of smoke and a tower of fire, as Amnon rides boasting upon the green fields, God shall tear his chariot-wheels with violent winds, and throw his body in the bloody sea. At him the thunder shall discharge its lightning bolt, and the thunder's fair spouse, the lightning bolt with bright and fiery wings, shall sit forever burning on Amnon's hateful bones. I myself, as swift as thunder or his spouse, will hunt an opportunity with a secret hate, to make sure that false Amnon has an ungracious end.

"Go to my house, my sister. Rest thyself in my house; and God in time shall take this shame from thee."

Thamar replied, "Neither God nor time will do that good for me."

CHAPTER 5

— Scene 5 —

In Jerusalem, King David and his train of attendants met David's son Absalom.

King David asked, "My Absalom, what are thou doing here alone, and why do thou bear such displeasure in thy brows?"

"Absalom has great cause to be displeased, and in his heart to shroud and conceal the wounds of wrath," Absalom replied.

"Against whom should Absalom be thus displeased?" King David asked.

Absalom replied, "Against wicked Amnon, thy ungracious son, my half-brother and fair Thamar's half-brother by the king, my step-brother by mother and by that part of his family: Amnon has dishonored David's holiness and affixed a blot of wanton evil on his throne, raping my sister Thamar when he feigned a sickness — a sickness sprung from the root of heinous lust."

King David asked, "Has Amnon brought this evil on my house, and has he allowed sin to smite his father's bones?

"Smite, David, deadlier than the voice of Heaven, and let hate's fire be kindled in thy heart. Flame in the arches of thy angry brows, making thy forehead, like a comet, glare, to cause false Amnon to tremble at thy looks."

The appearance of a comet in the sky was a malicious omen.

King David continued, "Sin, with his sevenfold crown and purple robe, begins his triumphs in my guilty throne."

Sin's sevenfold crown consists of the seven deadly sins: Lust, Gluttony, Greed, Sloth (Laziness), Wrath, Envy, and Pride.

King David was guilty of the sin of lust.

King David continued, "There he sits watching with his hundred eyes our idle minutes and our wanton thoughts, and with his tempting baits, made of our frail desires, gives us the hook that hauls our souls to Hell."

In Greek mythology, the giant Argus had one hundred eyes.

"But with the spirit of my kingdom's God, I'll thrust the flattering tyrant from his throne, and scourge his bond-slaves from my hallowed court with rods of iron and thorns of sharpened steel.

"So then, Absalom, don't thou revenge this sin. Leave it to me, and I will chasten Amnon."

"I am content," Absalom said.

Referring to King David in the third person, Absalom said to him, "Grant, my lord the king, that he himself with all his other lords would come up to my sheep-feast on the plain of Hazor."

The sheep-feast was part of a sheep-shearing festival.

King David said, "No, my fair son. I myself with all my lords will cause thee too much expense; yet some of my lords shall go."

Kings travel with large retinues. Feeding, sheltering, and entertaining all these people is expensive.

Absalom said, "But let my lord the king himself take pains to attend. The time of year is pleasant for your grace, and gladsome Summer in her shady robes, crowned with roses and with planted flowers, with all her nymphs, shall entertain my lord, and, from the thicket of my verdant groves, will sprinkle honey-dews about his breast, and cast sweet balm upon his kingly head.

"So grant thy servant's request, and go, my lord."

"Let it content my sweet son Absalom that I may stay in Jerusalem, and thou accept my other lords as your guests."

Absalom asked, "But shall thy best-beloved Amnon go?"

"Why do you want Amnon to go with thee?" King David asked.

"Yet do thy son and servant so much grace," Absalom requested, not answering the question.

"Amnon shall go, and all my other lords, because I will give grace to Absalom," King David replied.

Cusay and Uriah, with others, entered the scene.

Cusay said, "If it pleases my lord the king, his servant Joab has sent Uriah from the Syrian wars."

King David said, "Welcome, Uriah, from the Syrian wars. Welcome to David as his dearest lord."

Uriah replied, "Thanks be to Israel's God and God's grace that Uriah finds such greeting with the king."

Uriah was relieved that King David did not seem angry at him.

"No other greeting shall Uriah find as long as David governs in the chosen seat and consecrated throne of Israel," King David said.

King David had been elected — chosen — by God to succeed Saul as King of Israel.

He continued, "Tell me, Uriah, about my servant Joab. Does he with truth fight the battles of our God and for the honor of the Lord's anointed?"

King David was the Lord's anointed.

Uriah answered, "Thy servant Joab fights the chosen wars with truth, with honor, and with high success, and, against the wicked King of Ammon's sons, he has, by the finger — the power — of our sovereign's God, besieged the city of Rabbah, and taken control of the court of waters, where the conduits run, and of all the Ammonites' delightsome springs.

"Therefore he wishes that David's mightiness would raise soldiers in Israel, and come in person to the city of Rabbah, so that her conquest may be made the king's, and Joab fight as his subordinate."

King David said, "God and Joab's prowess has not done this without Uriah's valor, I am sure. Uriah, since his true conversion from a Hittite to an adopted son of Israel, has fought like one whose arms were lifted by Heaven, and whose bright sword was sharpened with Israel's wrath.

"Go, therefore, home, Uriah, and take thy rest. Visit thy wife and household with the joys that a victor and a favorite of the king's should exercise with honor after battle."

Uriah replied, "Thy servant's bones are not yet half so broken down, nor constituted on such a sickly and weak mold, that for so little service he should faint, and seek, as cowards do, the refuge of his home.

"Nor are his thoughts so sensually stirred by the thought of having sex with his wife that he would hold back the arms with which the Lord would use to smite Israel's enemies and fill their circle with his conquered foes, and instead enjoy the wanton bosom of a flattering wife."

King David had had sex with Bathsheba, and he was worried that she would become pregnant. Because Uriah had been away from his wife in order to fight for Israel, he would know that he was not the cause of the pregnancy. Therefore, King David wanted Uriah to have sex with Bathsheba so that if she became pregnant he would think that he had caused the pregnancy.

King David said, "Uriah has a beautiful and sober wife, yet young, and framed of tempting flesh and blood.

"So then, when the king has summoned thee from military service, if thou unkindly would refrain from joining with her in her bed, sin might be laid upon Uriah's soul, if Bathsheba by frailty hurt her reputation."

In other words, Bathsheba might commit adultery and lose her reputation if Uriah did not go home and satisfy her in bed.

King David continued, "So then go, Uriah, and take solace in her love. She whom God has knit to thee, tremble to loosen."

Uriah and Bathsheba were united by the knot of marriage; that marriage could fail if Uriah were to loosen the knot that united them.

Uriah replied, "The king is much too solicitous about my comfort. The Ark and Israel and Judah dwell in palaces and rich pavilions."

The Ark of the Covenant held the two stone tablets on which God had written with his finger the Ten Commandments.

Uriah continued, "But Joab and his brother dwell in the fields, suffering the wrath of winter and the sun: And shall Uriah (of more shame than they) banquet, and loiter in doing the work of Heaven?"

One of the seven deadly sins is sloth. One should be zealous in doing the work of God.

Uriah continued, "As surely as thy soul does live, my lord, my ears shall never lean to such delight, when holy labor calls me forth to fight."

King David said, "Then be it with Uriah's manly heart as best his reputation may shine in Israel."

Uriah replied, "Thus shall Uriah's heart be best content, until thou dismiss me back to Joab's bands.

"This ground before the king my master's doors shall be my couch, and this unwearied arm shall be the proper pillow of a soldier's head, for never will I lodge within my house, until Joab triumph in my secret vows."

He lay on the ground.

The secret vows were the ones that Uriah had just made. They were secret from Joab because he was not present to hear them. Uriah had vowed to return to Joab and help him triumph over the Ammonites.

King David ordered an attendant, "Fetch some flagons of our purest wine, so that we may welcome home our hardy friend with full carouses to his past fortunes and to the honors of his future arms."

Wine was usually mixed with water. Undiluted wine was a treat.

He continued, "Then I will send him back to the siege of Rabbah, and I will follow with the strength of Israel."

King David intended to raise soldiers and go to Rabbah and finish conquering it.

An attendant returned with flagons of wine.

King David said, "Arise, Uriah. Come and pledge the king."

Uriah said, "If David thinks that I am worthy of such a grace, I will be bold and pledge my lord the king."

He stood up.

King David said, "Both Absalom and Cusay shall drink to good Uriah and his happiness."

"We will, my lord, to please Uriah's soul," Absalom said.

King David said, "I will begin and make the first toast, Uriah. I drink to thyself and all the treasure of the Ammonites, which here I promise to impart to thee, and I bind that promise with a full draught."

King David drank.

Uriah said, "What seems pleasant in my sovereign's eyes, that Uriah shall do until he is dead."

King David ordered, "Fill his cup."

An attendant filled Uriah's cup with wine, and he drank.

King David then said, "Follow Uriah, you who love your sovereign's health, and do as he has done."

Absalom said, "May anyone who does not love David, or anyone who denies his authority, thrive badly and live poorly in Israel."

He then said, "Uriah, here is to the health of Abisai, Lord Joab's brother and thy loving friend."

Absalom drank.

Uriah said, "I pledge Lord Absalom and Abisai's health."

Uriah drank.

Cusay said, "Here now, Uriah, to the health of Joab, and to the pleasant journey we shall have when we return to the siege of mighty Rabbah."

Cusay drank.

Uriah said, "Cusay, I pledge thee all with all my heart."

Because his cup was empty, he said, "Give me some drink, you servants of the king. Give me my drink."

An attendant filled Uriah's cup with wine, and he drank.

King David said, "Well done, my good Uriah! Drink thy fill, so that David may rejoice in thy fullness."

By "thy fullness" King David meant Uriah's being full with wine. In different circumstances, the words could mean Uriah's being full of virtue.

"I will, my lord," Uriah answered.

Absalom said, "Now, Lord Uriah, drink one full draught to me."

"No, sir, I'll drink to the king," Uriah said. "Your father is a better man than you."

Uriah was becoming drunk. Some drunk people become rude.

"Do so, Uriah," King David said. "I will pledge thee immediately."

King David wanted Uriah to be drunker. Some drunk people do such things as forget their vows.

"I will, indeed, my lord and sovereign," Uriah said. "I'll for once in my days be so bold."

"Fill his glass," King David ordered.

"Fill my glass," Uriah said, giving an attendant his glass.

"Quickly, I say," King David said.

"Quickly, I say," Uriah said.

He was so drunk that he had started to repeat what others said.

He said, "Here, my lord, by your favor now I drink to you."

Uriah drank.

King David said, "I pledge thee, good Uriah, immediately."

King David drank.

Absalom said, "Here, then, Uriah, once again for me, and to the health of David's children."

Absalom drank.

"David's children!" Uriah said.

"Aye, David's children," Absalom said. "Will thou pledge me, man?"

"Pledge me, man!" Uriah said.

"Pledge me, I say," Absalom said, "or else thou don't love us."

"Do you talk? Do you talk?" Uriah said. "I'll drink no more; I'll lie down here."

King David said, "Instead of lying down here, Uriah, go home and sleep."

King David's purpose in getting Uriah drunk was to muddle his thinking so that he would forget his vows and go home to Bathsheba. If being drunk meant he wouldn't be able to have sex with her this night, he could have sex with her the next day.

"Oh, ho, sir!" Uriah said. "Would you make me break my vows?"

He lay down and said, "Home, sir! No, indeed, sir! I'll sleep upon my arm, like a soldier. I'll sleep like a man as long as I live in Israel."

King David thought, *If nothing will serve to save his wife's reputation, I'll send him with a letter to Joab to put him in the front lines of the wars, so my purposes may take effect.*

If Uriah were to serve in the front lines — the most dangerous position in battle — he could be killed and then King David would be able to marry Bathsheba.

King David ordered, "Help him in, sirs."

He and Absalom exited.

Cusay said, "Come, rise, Uriah. Get thee inside and sleep."

"I will not go home, sir," Uriah said. "That's for certain."

Cusay replied, "Then come and rest thyself upon David's bed."

"On, afore, my lords," Uriah said. "On, afore."

CHAPTER 6

— Chorus 1 —

The Chorus entered and criticized the evil behavior of King David:

"Oh, proud revolt of a presumptuous man, laying his bridle on the neck of sin, ready to bear him past his grave to Hell!"

King David was like a man getting on a horse that was ready to carry him to Hell.

"The death-prophesying raven, which in his voice carries the dreadful summons of our deaths, flies by the fair Arabian spices and Arabia's pleasant gardens and delightsome parks, seeming to curse them with his hoarse caws, and yet stoops with hungry violence to eat a piece of hateful carrion.

"Just like that raven, wretched man, displeased with those delights that would yield a quickening savor — a life-giving aroma — to his soul, pursues with eager and unquenched thirst the greedy longings of his loathsome flesh.

"If holy David has so shaken hands with sin, what shall our baser spirits glory in?

"This king who is giving lust her rein pursues the sequel with a greater ill.

"Uriah in the front lines of the wars has been murdered by the hateful heathens' sword, and David enjoys his too dear Bathsheba.

"Readers, know that this has happened, and that Bathsheba has given birth to a child, whose death the prophet solemnly does mourn."

After the death of Uriah, King David married Bathsheba, but the prophet Nathan rebuked King David because of his sin and predicted the death of his child who was conceived in adultery.

CHAPTER 7

— Scene 6 —

In the Royal Palace at Jerusalem, Bathsheba sat with her handmaid.

She said to herself, "Mourn, Bathsheba, bewail thy foolishness, thy sin, thy shame, the sorrow of thy soul. Sin, shame, and sorrow swarm about thy soul. And, in the gates and entrance of my heart, sadness, whose arms are most often wrapped around herself, hangs her lamentations. No comfort comes from the ten-stringed lyre, the twinkling cymbal, or the ivory lute, nor does the sound of David's kingly harp make glad the broken heart of Bathsheba.

"Jerusalem is filled with thy lamentations, and in the streets of Zion sits thy grief.

"The babe is sick, sick to the death, I fear, the fruit that sprung from thee to David's house; nor may the pot of honey and of oil gladden David or his handmaid's countenance."

By "handmaid," Bathsheba meant herself.

Deuteronomy 8:8 calls Israel "*a land wherein is oil olive and honey*" (1568 Bishop's Bible).

2 Kings 18:32 calls Israel "*a land of oil, of olive trees, and of honey*" (1568 Bishop's Bible).

Bathsheba continued, "Uriah — it causes me grief to think about him! For who among the sons of men does not say to my soul, 'The king has sinned, David has done amiss, and Bathsheba has laid snares of death to take Uriah's life'?

"My sweet Uriah, thou have fallen into the pit and gone even to the gates of Hell on account of Bathsheba, who would not shroud and conceal her shame.

"Oh, what is it to serve the lust of kings! How lion-like they rage when we resist!

"But, Bathsheba, in humbleness attend the grace that God will send to his handmaid."

CHAPTER 8

— Scene 7 —

King David, wearing loosely fitting clothing, walked sadly in a room in the palace at Jerusalem. Some attendants were present.

He said to himself, "The babe is sick, and sad is David's heart to see the guiltless bear the guilty's pain.

"David, hang up thy harp, hang down thy head, and dash thy ivory lute against the stones. The dew that falls on the hill of Hermon does not rain on Zion's tops and lofty towers. The plains of the Philistine cities Gath and Askaron rejoice, and David's thoughts are spent in pensiveness."

The Philistines were enemies of King David and Israel.

King David continued, "The babe is sick, sweet babe, whom Bathsheba with the woman's pain of childbirth brought forth to Israel."

The prophet Nathan entered the room.

King David asked, "But what has Nathan to say to his lord the king?"

The prophet replied, "Thus Nathan says to his lord the king: There were two men who were both dwellers in one town. The one was mighty, and exceedingly rich in oxen, sheep, and cattle of the field. The other was poor, having neither ox, nor calf, nor other animals, except for one little lamb that he had bought and nourished by hand. And it grew up, and fed with him and his family, and ate and drank as he and his family were accustomed to eat and drink, and in his bosom slept, and was to him as was his daughter or his dearest child. There came a stranger to this wealthy man, and the wealthy man refused to take one of his own animals or some of the abundance from his own storehouse to prepare and make the stranger food, but he took the poor man's sheep, which was a large part of the poor man's possessions, and prepared it for this stranger in his house.

"Tell me, what shall be done to the wealthy man for doing this?"

King David replied, "Now, as the Lord does live, this wicked man is judged and shall become the child of death. The wealthy man who without mercy took the poor man's lamb away shall restore fourfold to the poor man."

King David did not realize this, but Nathan the prophet had told a parable in which the wealthy man was King David, the poor man was Uriah, and the lamb was Bathsheba.

Nathan said to King David, "Thou are the man; and thou have judged thyself. David, thus says the Lord thy God by me:

"I anointed thee king in Israel, and saved thee from the tyranny of Saul. Thy master's house — his palace and kingdom — I gave thee to possess. His wives into thy bosom I did give to you, and Judah and Jerusalem I also did give to you. And, thou know, if this had been too little to give to you, I might have given thee more. Why, then, have thou gone so far astray, and have done evil, and sinned in my sight? Thou have killed Uriah with the sword. Yes, with the sword of the uncircumcised thou have slain him. For that reason, from this day forth, the sword shall never go from thee and thine, for thou have taken this Hittite's wife to thee. For this reason, behold, I will, says Jacob's God, in thine own house stir evil up to thee. Yes, I before thy face will take thy wives, and give them to thy neighbor to possess. This shall be done to David in the light of day, so that Israel openly may see thy shame."

King David said, "Nathan, I have sinned against the Lord, I have. Oh, I have sinned grievously! And, lo, from Heaven's throne David does throw himself and groan and grovel to the gates of Hell!"

He fell down.

Raising him, Nathan the prophet said, "David, stand up. Thus says the Lord by me: *David the king shall live, for he has seen the true repentant sorrow of thy heart.*

"But, because thou have in this misdeed of thine stirred up the enemies of Israel to triumph, and to blaspheme the God of Hosts, and say that he set a wicked man to reign over his loved people and his tribes — the child

shall surely die, that earlier was born, his mother's sin, his kingly father's disgrace."

Nathan the prophet exited.

King David said to himself, "How just is Jacob's God in all his works! But must the babe die that David loves so?

"Oh, the Mighty One of Israel will not change His judgment, and says the babe must die!

"Mourn, Israel, and weep in the gates of Zion. Wither, you cedar-trees of Lebanon; you sprouting almonds, with your flowering tops, droop, drown, and drench in Hebron's fearful streams."

The word "drench" meant to sink in water.

King David continued, "The babe must die who was to David born, his mother's sin, his kingly father's disgrace."

He sadly sat down.

Cusay entered the room.

The first servant asked Cusay, "What tidings does Cusay bring to the king?"

Cusay said, "To thee, the servant of King David's court, this is the news that Cusay brings. Just as the prophet prophesized, the Lord has surely stricken to the death the newborn child given birth to by the wife of Uriah, who by the sons of Ammon was earlier slain."

"Cusay, be quiet," the first servant said. "The king is sorely vexed. How shall the person who first brings this news fare, when, while the child was yet alive, we spoke, and David's heart would not be comforted?"

Overhearing these last few words, King David said, "Yes, David's heart will not be comforted! What are you murmuring, you servants of the king? What news does Cusay have to tell to the king? Tell me, Cusay, is the child still living, or is he dead?"

Cusay answered, "The child is dead whom David fathered with Uriah's wife."

"Uriah's wife, say thou?" King David said.

He paused and then said, "The child is dead, so then David's shame ceases."

King David would never have to look at the child as the child grew, and so he therefore would no longer be reminded of his sin and shame were he to look at the child.

King David then said, "Fetch me food to eat, and give me wine to drink, water to wash, and oil to rub on my skin to clear my looks.

"Bring down your shalms, your cymbals, and your pipes."

All of these items were musical instruments.

He continued, "Let David's harp and lute, his hand and voice, give praise to Him who loves Israel, and sing the praise of Him who defended David's reputation, who put away his sin from out of his sight, and sent his shame into the streets of Gath."

Gath was the home of some of his and Israel's enemies; they would rejoice when hearing of King David's shame.

King David continued, "Bring to me the mother of the babe, so that I may wipe the tears from off her face, and give her comfort with this hand of mine, and dress fair Bathsheba in beautiful clothing, so that she may bear to me another son who may be loved by the Lord of Hosts.

"For where my dead son is, David must necessarily go, but never may my dead son come where David is now."

Some attendants brought in water, wine, and olive oil. They also brought in musical instruments and a banquet of food.

Bathsheba entered the room.

King David said to her, "Fair Bathsheba, sit thou, and sigh no more."

He ordered the servants, "Sing and play, you servants of the king. Now David's sorrow sleeps with the dead, and Bathsheba lives to Israel."

They ate, drank, and sang.

King David said, "Now prepare at once weapons and warlike engines for assault, you men of Israel, you men of Judah and Jerusalem, so that Rabbah may be taken by the king, lest it be called after Joab's name and David's glory will not shine in the streets of Zion.

"To Rabbah King David marches with his men, in order to chastise Ammon and the wicked ones."

CHAPTER 9

The sheep-feast was occurring. Amnon was present at the sheep-feast, and he was the master of the feast, but Absalom and many men who obeyed his orders were also present at the sheep-feast.

Absalom had wanted Amnon to attend his sheep-feast, but instead he was attending Amnon's sheep-feast.

Or perhaps this was Absalom's sheep-feast, and he was honoring Amnon by making him the master of the feast.

Either way, Absalom had a malicious purpose hidden in his heart.

Absalom and several of his men stood together in a field.

Absalom said to them, "Set up your mules and give them good provender to eat, and let us meet our brothers at the feast.

"Accursed is the master of this feast. He is the dishonor of the house of Israel, he is the cause of his half-sister's loss of reputation, and he is his mother's shame.

"Shame be the share of him who could such ill contrive, to rape Thamar, and, without a pause, to drive her shamefully out of his house.

"But may his wickedness find just reward! Therefore, Absalom conspires with you to bring it about that Amnon dies at whatever time he sits to eat, for in the holy temple I have sworn to get revenge for his villainy in Thamar's rape."

Seeing Amnon and some others coming toward them, he said, "And here he comes. All of you, speak gently to him, this man whose death is deeply engraved in my heart.

Amnon, Adonia, and Jonadab came over to Absalom and his followers. Amnon and Adonia were two of King David's sons. Jonadab was King David's nephew and a close friend to Amnon.

Amnon said, "Our shearers are not far from here, I know, and Amnon to you, all his brethren, gives such welcome as our fathers formerly were accustomed to give in Judah and Jerusalem."

He then said, "But, especially, Lord Absalom, Amnon gives welcome to thee, the honor of thy house and progeny. Sit down and dine with me, King David's son, thou fair young man, whose hairs shine in my eye like the golden wires of David's ivory lute."

Absalom asked, "Amnon, where are thy shearers and thy men, so that we may pour in us plenty of thy wines, and eat thy goats'-milk, and rejoice with thee?"

Amnon replied, "Here come Amnon's shearers and his men. Absalom, sit and rejoice with me."

A company of shepherds arrived and danced and sang.

Amnon said, "Drink, Absalom, in praise of Israel. Welcome to Amnon's fields from David's court."

Stabbing Amnon as he drank, Absalom said, "Die with thy draught; perish, and die accursed, you dishonor to the honor of us all. Die for the villainy you did to Thamar. You are unworthy to be King David's son!"

With Amnon dead, Absalom exited with his followers.

Jonadab, Amnon's good friend, said, "Oh, what has Absalom done for Thamar? He has murdered his half-brother, great King David's son!"

Adonia said, "Run away, Jonadab, and make it known what cruelty this Absalom has shown to Amnon."

He then said to Amnon's corpse, "Amnon, thy brother Adonia shall bury thy body among other dead men's bones, and we will grieve as we tell Israel about Amnon's death and Absalom's pride."

Absalom was proud because he had punished Amnon instead of allowing King David to do it, as King David had wanted.

CHAPTER 10

— Scene 9 —

Outside the walls of Rabbah, the capital city of the Ammonites, stood King David, Joab, Abisai, Cusay, and others, including a drummer and an ensign carrying the army's banner.

King David said, "This is Rabbah, the town of the uncircumcised, the city of the kingdom, where wicked Hanon sits as king. Rob this king, this Hanon of his crown. Unpeople Rabbah and the streets thereof. Kill everyone, for in their blood and the slaughter of the slain lies the honor of King David's line. Joab, Abisai, and the rest of you, fight this day for great Jerusalem."

The Ammonite King Hanon and others appeared on the walls of Rabbah.

Joab said, "See where Hanon shows himself on the walls. Why, then, do we refrain from assaulting the city so that Israel may, as it is promised, subdue the daughters of the Gentiles' tribes? All this must be performed by David's hand."

King David said, "Listen to me, Hanon, and remember well. As surely as He does live who kept my army safe, at that time our young men, by the pool of Gibeon, went forth against the strength of Isboseth, and twelve to twelve did with their weapons play, so surely are thou and thy men of war to feel the sword of Israel this day, because thou have defied Jacob's God, and allowed Rabbah with the Philistine allies to rail upon and insult the tribe of Benjamin."

After King Saul of Israel died, Isboseth — his son — and David contended for the throne of Israel. They met by the city of Gibeon and agreed that twenty-four men — twelve men from each side — would fight to decide who would become King of Israel. All twenty-four warriors were killed, and then the two sides engaged in a full-out battle, with David's army earning the victory.

King Hanon replied, "Listen, man. As surely as Saul thy master fell, and gored his sides upon the mountain-tops, and Jonathan, Abinadab, and Melchisua, watered the dales and deeps of Askaron with bloody streams that from Gilboa ran in channels through the wilderness of Ziph, at that time the sword of the uncircumcised was drunken with the blood of Israel, so surely shall David perish with his men under the walls of Rabbah, Hanon's town."

The Philistines had defeated the Israelites at Mount Gilboa. Seeing that the Israelites were losing the battle, Saul committed suicide by falling on his sword.

Joab said, "Hanon, the God of Israel has said, *David the king shall wear that crown of thine that weighs a talent of the finest gold, and triumph in the spoil of Hanon's town, when Israel shall hale thy people hence, and turn them to the tile-kiln, man and child, and put them under harrows made of iron, and hew their bones with axes, and their limbs with iron swords divide and tear in twain.*"

King David had ordered the Israelites to kill all the citizens of Rabbah following the forthcoming victory. Some would be baked in ovens for baking tiles. Some would have their flesh torn from their bodies by having harrows dragged over them. Some would be cut to pieces with swords.

2 Samuel 12:30-31 (1568 Bishop's Bible) described what happened after King David was victorious:

30 And he took their king's crown from off his head (which weighed a talent of gold, and in it were precious stones) and it was set on David's head, and he brought away the people of the city, in exceeding great abundance.

31 And he carried away the people that was therein, and put them under saws and under iron harrows, and under axes of iron, and thrust them into the tile-kiln: thus did he with all the cities of the children of Ammon. And so David and all the people returned to Jerusalem.

By "put them under saws" is meant "sawed them to death."

1 Chronicles 20:3 states, "*And he brought out the people that were in it, and tormented them with saws and harrows of iron, and with other sharp instruments, and so dealt David with all the cities of the children of Ammon: And David and all the people came again to Jerusalem*" (1568 Bishop's Bible).

(Many translations of the Bible say that King David set the conquered people to work with these implements and to work in the tile-kiln.)

Joab said, "Hanon, this shall be done to thee and thine because thou have defied Israel."

He then ordered his troops, "To arms, to arms, so that Rabbah feels revenge, and Hanon's town becomes King David's spoil!"

They fought the battle, and the Israelite army was victorious. Hanon was killed in the battle.

Wearing the late King Hanon's crown, King David met with Joab, Abisai, Cusay, and other Israelites.

King David said, "Now clattering arms and wrathful storms of war have thundered over Rabbah's razed, pulled-down towers. The avenging ire of great Jehovah's arm made the gates of Rabbah to open for His people, and clothed the cherubim in fiery coats to fight against the wicked Hanon's town.

"Pay thanks, you men of Judah, to the King, the God of Zion and Jerusalem, Who has exalted and raised Israel to this, and crowned David with this diadem."

Joab said, "As beauteous and bright is he among the tribes as when the sun, attired in his shiny, glittering robe, comes dancing from his oriental, eastern gate and hurls like a bridegroom his radiant beams through the gloomy air. Like such does King David appear, crowned with the honor of his enemies' town, shining in riches like the firmament, the starry vault that overhangs the earth — so appears David, King of Israel."

Abisai said, "Joab, why doesn't David mount his throne, David, whom Heaven has beautified with Hanon's crown? Sound trumpets, shalms, and instruments of praise, to Jacob's God for David's victory."

The musical instruments sounded.

Having traveled from the place of Amnon's murder, Jonadab entered the scene.

Jonadab said, "Why does the King of Israel rejoice? Why sits David crowned with Rabbah's rule? Behold, there has great sorrow befallen in Amnon's fields because of the evil deed of Absalom. Absalom has overturned with his sword Amnon's shearers and their feast of mirth, nor do any of King David's sons live to bring these bitter tidings to the king."

Jonadab was incorrect when he said that none of King David's sons were alive to carry the news to him. Absalom had killed only Amnon. Jonadab may have been afraid that after he left, Absalom had returned and had killed David's son Adonia and David's other sons.

King David said, "Evil hurts me! How soon are David's triumphs dashed, how suddenly declines David's pride! As the daylight sets and diminishes in the west, so dims David's glory and his magnificence. Die, David, for to thee is left no seed who may revive thy name in Israel."

Without sons to succeed him as King of Israel, his name could be lost to memory and history.

Seeing Adonia and some of King David's other sons coming toward them, Jonadab said: "In Israel some of David's seed is left."

Perhaps Amnon had been killed in Judah, and perhaps Jonadab had earlier meant that none of David's sons in Judah were still alive.

Jonadab said to the people around King David, "Comfort your lord, you servants of the king."

He then said to King David, "Behold, thy sons return in mourning clothing, and Absalom has slain only Amnon."

Adonia and some other sons of King David entered the scene.

King David said, "Welcome, my sons. You are dearer to me than is this golden crown or Hanon's spoil.

"Oh, tell me, then, tell me, my sons, I say, how came it to pass that Absalom has slain his brother Amnon with the sword?"

Adonia replied, "Oh, king, thy sons went up to Amnon's fields to feast with him and eat his bread and oil, and Absalom upon his mule came, and to his men he said, 'When Amnon's heart is merry and secure, then strike him dead because he raped Thamar shamefully, and hated her, and threw her out of his doors.' This he did, and they with him conspired and killed thy son Absalom to get revenge for the wrong done to Thamar."

King David asked, "How long shall Judah and Jerusalem grieve and water Zion with their tears! How long shall Israel lament in vain, and not a man among the mighty ones will hear the sorrows of King David's heart!

"Amnon, thy life was as pleasing to thy lord as to my ears is the music of my lute, or songs that David tunes to his harp, and Absalom has taken away from me the gladness of my sad distressed soul."

Joab and some others exited.

Following the murder of Amnon, Absalom went into exile and stayed with his grandfather Talmai, the king of Geshur.

A woman from the town of Thecoa, which was about ten miles from Jerusalem, arrived and stood before King David.

The woman of Thecoa knelt and said, "God save King David, King of Israel, and bless the gates of Zion for his sake!"

King David said to her, "Woman, why do thou mourn? Rise up from the earth. Tell me what sorrow has befallen thy soul."

The woman of Thecoa rose and said, "Oh, king, thy servant's soul is sorely troubled, and grievous is the anguish of her heart. From Thecoa has thy handmaid — thy servant — come."

King David said, "Tell me, thou woman of Thecoa, what ails thee and what has happened."

The woman of Thecoa replied, "Thy servant is a widow in Thecoa. Two sons thy handmaid had, and they, my lord, fought in the field, and no man went between them to stop the fight, and so the one did smite and slay the other.

"And then the relatives of my sons arose and cried against the one who smote his brother, wanting him therefore to be the child of death and saying, 'For we will follow and destroy the heir.'"

In other words, the relatives wanted to kill the living son to avenge the killing of the other son.

She continued, "So they will quench that sparkle that is left, and leave neither name nor children on the earth to me or to thy handmaid's dead husband."

King David said, "Woman, return; go home to thy house. I will give the command that thy son shall be safe. If any man say that thy son shall be otherwise than well, bring him to me, and I shall chastise him, for I swear that as the Lord does live, not a hair shall shed from thy son or fall upon the earth. Woman, to God alone belongs revenge. Shall, then, the relatives slay thy living son for his sin?"

King David did not realize this, but the woman of Thecoa had told a parable in which the two sons were Absalom and Amnon, and the relatives included King David.

The woman of Thecoa said, "King David has spoken well to his handmaid. But why, then, have thou determined so hard a part against the righteous tribes, to follow and pursue the banished, when to God alone belongs revenge? Assuredly thou have spoken against thyself. Therefore, call home again the banished. Call home the banished so that he may live, and raise to thee some fruit in Israel."

She was asking that Absalom be allowed to return to Israel and father some children.

An intelligent man, King David said, "Thou woman of Thecoa, answer me one thing I shall ask of thee: Isn't the hand of Joab in this action? Tell me, isn't his finger in this deed?"

The woman of Thecoa replied, "It is, my lord; his hand is in this deed. Assure thyself that Joab, captain of thy army, has put these words into thy handmaid's mouth, and thou are as an angel from on high to understand the meaning of my heart.

"Look, Joab is coming to his lord the king."

Joab wanted to reconcile King David and his son Absalom. As a military man, Joab knew that if the two men remained unreconciled, Absalom could decide to raise an army, oust David, and become King of Israel. Chances of that happening were much less if the two men were reconciled, although it could still happen if Absalom were ambitious.

Joab entered the scene.

King David said, "Tell me, Joab, did thou send this woman in to tell me this parable in behalf of Absalom?"

Referring to himself in the third person, Joab said, "My lord, Joab did ask this woman to speak. And she has spoken, and thou have understood."

King David replied, "I have, and I am content to do the thing you want me to do. Go and fetch my son, so that he may live with me."

Joab knelt and said, "Now God be blessed for King David's life! Thy servant Joab has found grace with thee, in that thou are sparing Absalom, thy child."

He stood up and said about Absalom, "He is a beautiful and fair young man. In all his body no blemish is seen. His hair that twines about his bright and ivory-white neck is like the wires of David's harp. In Israel there is not such a splendid man, and here I bring him to entreat you for grace."

Joab brought in Absalom to see King David.

King David started to upbraid Absalom for murdering Amnon: "Did thou slain Amnon in the fields of Hazor —"

But then he stopped and rejoiced that Absalom had returned to Israel: "— ah, Absalom, my son. Ah, my son, Absalom!

"But why do I vex thy spirit so? Live, and return from Gesur to thy house. Return from Gesur to Jerusalem. What good does it do for me to be bitter to thy soul? Amnon is dead, and Absalom survives."

Absalom said, "Father, I have offended Israel, and I have offended David and his house. To avenge the wrong done to Thamar, Absalom has done wrong.

"But David's heart is free from sharp revenge, and Joab has gotten grace for Absalom."

King David said, "Depart with me, you men of Israel, you who have followed Rabbah with the sword, and ransack Ammon's richest treasuries."

He then said, "Live, Absalom, my son, live once more in peace. Peace be with thee, and with Jerusalem!"

Everyone except Absalom exited.

Absalom said to himself, "David is gone, and Absalom remains, flowering in the pleasant springtime of his youth."

But he was ambitious, and his ambition was unfulfilled.

He said, "Why does Absalom live without being honored by the tribes and elders and the mightiest ones, so that round about his temples he may wear garlands and wreaths set on him with respect so that everyone who has a cause to plead might come to Absalom and call for right?

"Then in the gates of Zion I would sit, and publish laws in great Jerusalem, and not a man would live in all the land unless Absalom would do him reason's due.

"Therefore I shall address me, as I may, to love the men and tribes of Israel."

Absalom was thinking ahead. He would become a judge and resolve disputes. By settling disputes in favor of the northern tribes, he would become influential among them, and when he wanted them to, they would follow him.

CHAPTER 11

— Scene 10 —

King David, Ithay, Sadoc, Ahimaas, Jonathan, and others met on the Mount of Olives.

Ithay, a military captain from Gath, commanded 600 soldiers. Although Gath was a Philistine city, when David was a young man, Ithay's father, the King of Gath, had been kind to him.

Sadoc was a high priest, and Ahimaas was his son. Abiathar was a priest, and Jonathan was his son.

King David was barefoot, with some loose covering over his head, and all of them were mourning.

Absalom had raised an army and was rebelling against his father. King David had fled Jerusalem with some followers, and he and they were mourning on the Mount of Olives east of Jerusalem.

King David said, "Proud lust, the bloodiest traitor to our souls, whose greedy throat not earth, not air, not sea, and not Heaven can glut or satisfy with any abundance, thou are the causes for these torments that suck my blood, piercing with the venom of thy poisoned eyes the strength and marrow of my tainted bones."

The lust could be King David's sexual lust for Bathsheba, or Absalom's lust for power, or both.

King David then described God's parting of the Red Sea to save the Jews and to punish the Jews' enemies: "To punish Pharaoh and his cursed army, the waters shrunk at great Adonai's voice, and the sandy bottom of the sea appeared, offering his service at his servant's feet."

He continued, "And, to inflict a plague on David's sin, He makes his bowels traitors to his breast, winding about his heart with deadly grip.

"Ah, Absalom, the wrath of Heaven inflames thy scorched bosom with ambitious heat, and Satan sets thee on a tower of lust, showing thy thoughts the pride of Israel, of choice to cast thee on her ruthless stones!"

Satan was tempting Absalom with power over Israel, but he was tempting Absalom only so that he could destroy Absalom.

King David continued, "Weep with me, then, ye sons of Israel. Lie down with David, and with David mourn before the Holy One Who sees our hearts."

King David lay down on the ground, as did all the others with him.

He continued, "And fill the face of every flower with the dew of your tears. Season this heavy soil with showers of tears. Weep, Israel, for David's soul dissolves into tears, filling the fountains of his drowned eyes and pours her tears on the unfeeling earth."

Sadoc, high priest of the Israelites, said, "Weep, Israel. Oh, weep for David's soul, strewing the ground with hair and torn garments to serve as the tragic witness of your hearty woes!"

While mourning, ancient people would sometimes cut off some of their hair. They would also tear their clothing.

Ahimaas, Sadoc's son, said, "Oh, I wish our eyes were conduits to our hearts, and I wish that our hearts were seas of liquid blood, to pour in streams upon this holy mountain, to serve as witness that we would die for David's woes!"

Jonathan, the son of the priest Abiathar, said, "Then this Mount of Olives would seem to be a plain drowned with a sea, which with our sighs should roar, and, in the murmur of its mounting waves, would report our bleeding sorrows to the heavens as witness we would die for David's woes."

Ithay, a military captain from Gath, said, "Earth cannot weep enough for David's woes. Then weep, you heavens, and, all you clouds, dissolve into drops of tears, so that piteous stars may see our miseries, and drop their golden tears upon the ground to serve as witness how they weep for David's woes."

Sadoc the high priest said, "Now let my sovereign raise his prostrate bones, and mourn not as a faithless man would do, but let him be assured that Jacob's righteous God, Who promised never to forsake your throne, will still be just and pure in his vows."

King David said, "Sadoc, high priest, preserver of the Ark of the Covenant, whose sacred virtue keeps the chosen crown, I know my God is spotless in His vows, and that these hairs shall greet my grave in peace.

"But that my son would wrong his tendered soul, and fight against his father's happiness, turns all my hopes into despair of him, and that despair feeds all my veins with grief."

Ithay, the military captain from Gath, said, "Think of it, David, as a fatal plague that grief preserves, but does not prevent, and turn thy drooping eyes upon the troops that, because of their affection for thy worthiness, swarm about the person of the king. Cherish their valor and their zealous love with pleasant looks and sweet encouragements."

King David said, "I think the voice of Ithay fills my ears."

Ithay replied, "Don't let the voice of Ithay be hateful to thine ears. Ithay's heart would soothe thy bosom with his tears."

King David asked why Ithay and his soldiers were loyal to him: "But why do thou go to the wars with us? Thou are a stranger here in Israel, and thou are a son of Achis, the mighty King of Gath. Therefore return to Gath, and stay with thy father. Thou came to me only yesterday. Should I now let thee partake in these troubles here with us? Keep both thyself and all thy soldiers safe. Let me abide the hazards of these battles, and may God requite the friendship thou have shown to me."

Ithay replied, "As surely as Israel's God gives David life, whatever place or peril shall contain or threaten David the king, the same will Ithay share in life and death. I will go wherever you will go, and I will share whatever danger you face."

King David said, "Then, gentle Ithay, be thou still with us, a joy to David, and a grace to Israel."

He then spoke to Sadoc, who had taken the Ark of the Covenant with him when fleeing from Jerusalem:

"Go, Sadoc, now, and bear the Ark of God into great Jerusalem again. If I find favor in God's gracious eyes, then He will lay his hand upon my heart yet once again before I visit death, giving it strength, and giving virtue to my eyes, to taste the comforts and behold the form of his fair Ark of the Covenant and holy tabernacle.

"But if he should say, *My wonted love is worn, and I have no delight in David now*, then here lie I armed with a humble heart to embrace the pains that anger shall impose, and kiss the sword my lord shall kill me with.

"Sadoc, take thy son Ahimaas, and Jonathan the son of Abiathar, with you when you return to Jerusalem, and in these fields I will rest until they return from you some certain news."

Sadoc, Ahimaas, and Jonathan would serve as spies for King David in Jerusalem.

Sadoc replied, "Thy servants will with joy obey the king and hope to cheer his heart with happy news."

Sadoc, Ahimaas, and Jonathan exited.

Ithay said to King David, "Now that it shall be no grief to the king, let me for good inform his majesty that, with unkind-to-kindred and graceless Absalom, Achitophel your ancient counselor directs the state of this rebellion."

Achitophel, one of King David's counselors, had gone over to the side of Absalom and was advising him.

King David said, "Then does it — Achitophel's advice — aim with danger at my crown."

He knelt and prayed, "Oh, Thou, Who holds His raging bloody boundary within the circle of the silver moon, Who girds Earth's center with His watery scarf, limit the counsel of Achitophel, no bounds extending to my soul's distress, but turn his wisdom into foolishness!"

God's raging bloody boundary was the circle of the silver moon, which meant that God's raging bloody territory included the entire Earth. God's watery scarf was the ocean, which wrapped around the Earth like a scarf.

King David was praying that God would limit Achitophel's counsel, which should be wise, so that it would not hurt King David. He wanted Achitophel's counsel to be that of a foolish, not a wise, man.

Cusay entered the scene. His coat was torn, and his head was covered with dust.

In ancient times, grieving people sometimes poured dust on their head.

Cusay said, "Happiness and honor to my lord the king!"

King David replied, "What happiness or honor may betide the state of him who toils in my dangers and extreme circumstances?"

Cusay replied, "Oh, let my gracious sovereign cease these griefs, unless he wishes his servant Cusay to die — Cusay's life depends upon my lord's relief!

"Let my presence with my sighs perfume the pleasant repository of my sovereign's soul."

Cusay wanted to do King David's mourning for him.

"No, Cusay, no," King David said. "Thy presence to me will be a burden, since I care for thee and cannot endure thy sighs for David's sake. But if thou return to fair Jerusalem, and say to Absalom that just as thou have been a trusty friend to his father's seat, so thou will be to him, and call him king, Achitophel's counsel may be brought to naught."

King David wanted Cusay to pretend to serve Absalom but to give bad advice that would counter Achitophel's good advice.

King David continued, "Then along with Sadoc and Abiathar, thou and they may learn the secrets of my son, and thou can send to me messages by Ahimaas and friendly Jonathan, who both are there in Jerusalem."

Cusay replied, "Then rise, and trust God with the outcome of these actions."

"Cusay, I rise," King David said, "although with unwieldy bones I carry weapons against my Absalom."

CHAPTER 12

— Scene 11 —

In the palace in Jerusalem were Absalom, Amasa, and Achitophel, along with the concubines of David. Others were also present. Everyone was very well dressed, and Absalom had been crowned.

Amasa was King David's nephew; he was the son of David's sister Abigail. He was also the captain of Absalom's army.

Absalom said, "Now you who were my father's concubines, liquor to his unchaste and lustful fire, have seen his honor shaken in his house, which I possess in the sight of all the world. I bring you forth as foils to my renown, and to eclipse the glory of your king, whose life is with his honor fast enclosed within the entrails of a jet-black cloud, whose dissolution into rain shall pour down in showers the substance of his life and swelling pride."

A foil is a thin piece of metal put under a jewel to show it off to better effect.

By taking possession of King David's concubines, Absalom was showing off his power.

He continued, "Then shall the stars light earth with rich aspects, and Heaven shall burn in love with Absalom, whose beauty will suffice to chase away all mists, and clothe the sun's sphere with a triple fire, sooner than his clear eyes should suffer stain, or be offended with a lowering day."

Absalom was saying that his beauty outshone the fire of the Sun by three times.

King David's concubines quickly showed that they remained loyal to him.

The first concubine said, "Thy father's honor, graceless Absalom, and ours thus beaten with thy violent arms, will cry for vengeance to the Host of Heaven, whose power is always and forever armed against the proud, and will dart plagues at thy aspiring head for doing this disgrace to David's throne."

The Host of Heaven is the armies of angels under God.

The second concubine picked up where the first concubine left off:

"— to David's throne, to David's holy throne, whose scepter angels guard with swords of fire, and sit as eagles on his conquering fist, ready to prey upon his enemies.

"So then don't think that thou, the captain of his foes, even if thou were much swifter than Azahell was, who could outrun the nimble-footed roe, to escape the fury of their thumping beaks or the dreadful reach of their commanding wings."

Azahell, the brother of Joab and Abisai, had died in the Battle at Gibeon.

Achitophel advised, "Let not my lord the King of Israel be angry with a silly woman's threats, but with the pleasure he has earlier enjoyed, let him turn them back to their private quarters again until David's conquest becomes their overthrow."

Absalom said, "Into your bowers, you daughters of disdain, begotten by the fury of unbridled lust, and wash your couches with your mourning tears, for grief that David's kingdom is decayed and ruined."

The first concubine said, "No, Absalom, King David's kingdom is chained fast to the finger of great Jacob's God, Who will not loosen it for a rebel's love."

The concubines exited.

Amasa said to Absalom, "If I might give advice to the king, these concubines should buy their taunts with blood."

He was advising that the concubines be killed.

"Amasa, no," Absalom replied, "but let thy martial sword empty the veins of David's armed men, and let these foolish women escape our hands to recompense the shame they have sustained."

As concubines, they served the king's lust.

2 Samuel 16:22 states, "*And so they spread a tent upon the top of the house, and Absalom went in unto his father's concubines in the sight of all Israel*" (1568 Bishop's Bible).

Absalom continued, "First, Absalom was by the trumpet's sound proclaimed throughout Hebron King of Israel, and now he is set in fair Jerusalem with complete state and the glory of a crown. Fifty fair footmen by my chariot run, and to the air whose rupture rings my fame, wherever I ride, they offer reverence and veneration.

"Why shouldn't Absalom, who in his face carries the final purpose of his God, which is to work him grace in Israel, endeavor to achieve with all his strength the magnificence that most may satisfy his joy, keeping his statutes and his covenants pure?"

So Absalom said. One wonders *who* would work *him* grace in Israel. Was Absalom going to work God grace in Israel, or was God going to work Absalom grace in Israel? Would Absalom serve God, or would God serve Absalom?

Absalom continued, "His thunder is entangled in my hair, and with my beauty is His lightning quenched."

Absalom was vain.

He continued, "I am the man he made to glory in, when by the errors of my father's sin David lost the path that led into the land with which our chosen ancestors were blessed."

Cusay, whom King David had sent to be his undercover agent, entered the throne room and said to Absalom, whom he called "king" without meaning it, "Long may the beautiful King of Israel live, to whom the people do by the thousands swarm!"

Absalom asked, "Why does Cusay so greet his foe? Is this the love thou show to David's soul, to whose assistance thou have vowed thy life? Why do thou leave him in this emergency?"

Cusay replied, "Because the Lord and Israel have chosen thee. As I have previously served thy father's turn with counsel acceptable in his sight, so likewise I will now serve and obey his son."

Absalom said, "Then welcome, Cusay, to King Absalom."

He then said, "And now, my lords and loving counselors, I think it is time to exercise our arms and do battle against forsaken David and his army.

"Give counsel first, my good Achitophel, and say what times and orders we may best observe for the prosperous management of these high exploits."

Achitophel said, "Let me choose out twelve thousand valiant men, and, while the night hides with her sable mists the close endeavors cunning soldiers use, I will assault thy discontented sire, and, while with weakness of their weary arms, overwhelmed with toil, David's people flee in huge disordered troops to escape from the sudden attack of thy army in order to save their lives, and leave the king alone, then I will smite him with his last and final wound, and bring the people to thy feet in peace."

His advice was good. He would quickly raise twelve thousand soldiers and attack King David and his weary soldiers in a surprise attack at night. These twelve thousand soldiers would be enough to rout David's army, and in the confusion, when David was not protected, Achitophel would kill him.

Absalom said, "Well has Achitophel given his advice. Yet let us hear the counsel of Cusay, whose great experience is well worth hearing."

King David had sent Cusay to Absalom to give him bad advice that would counter the good advice of Achitophel.

Referring to Absalom as his "king," Cusay said, "Although wise Achitophel is much more fitting to purchase hearing with my lord the king, on account of all his former counsels, than myself, yet, not offending Absalom or him, this time is not good for nor worth pursuit of David, for, as well thou know, thy father's men are strong, and they are as enraged as she-bears are that have been robbed of their cubs. Besides, the king himself is a valiant man, trained and educated in the feats and stratagems of war, and he will not, in order to prevent the worst that could happen — his death — lodge with the common soldiers in the field.

"But now, I know, his accustomed policies have taught him to lurk within some secret cave, guarded with all his bravest soldiers, who if the forefront of his army grow faint, will yet give out that Absalom flees, and so discourage thy soldiers."

Even if Absalom's soldiers were to defeat those of David's soldiers in the front ranks, David's bravest soldiers would spread the false news that it was Absalom's soldiers who were being defeated. This would help rally David's soldiers and could cause Absalom's soldiers to grow faint.

Cusay continued, "David himself, also, whose angry heart is as a lion's annoyed in his walk, will fight, and all his men to a man will fight, before a few shall vanquish him by fear.

"My counsel therefore is, with trumpet's sound to gather men throughout Israel, from the settlement of Dan in the north to the town of Bersabe in the south, so that they may march in numbers like those of sea-sands that nestle close to one another's neck. So shall we come upon him in our strength, like the dew that falls in showers from Heaven, and we will leave him not a man to march with."

Cusay advised gathering a vast army of soldiers — as numerous as the grains of sand — from the men throughout Israel and then attacking David with overwhelming force.

Cusay's advice would help David by keeping him from being attacked and defeated quickly. At this time, twelve thousand soldiers would be enough to defeat him with a surprise attack at night.

Cusay continued, "Besides, if any city succor David, the numbers of our men shall fetch ropes for us, and we will pull the city down the river's stream, so that not a stone is left to keep us out."

Absalom asked Amasa, the leader of his army, "What says my lord to Cusay's counsel now?"

Amasa said, "I fancy Cusay's counsel far better than the advice that Achitophel gave us, and so, I think, does every soldier here."

The soldiers present said, "Cusay's counsel is better than Achitophel's."

Absalom said, "Then march we all after Cusay's counsel: We will follow his advice.

"Sound trumpets through the territory of Israel, and muster all the men to serve the king, so that Absalom may glut his longing soul with the sole possession of his father's crown."

Achitophel thought, *Ill shall they fare who follow the military expeditions of you, who scorn the counsel of Achitophel.*

Everyone except Cusay exited.

Cusay said to himself, "Thus has the power of Jacob's jealous God fulfilled his servant David's plan through me, and brought Achitophel's advice to scorn."

Sadoc, Abiathar, Ahimaas, and Jonathan entered. All of these served King David, although like Cusay, they pretended to serve Absalom.

Sadoc the high priest said, "God save Lord Cusay and direct his zeal to obtain David's conquest against his son!"

Abiathar the priest asked Cusay, "What secrets have thou gleaned from Absalom?"

"Sacred priests that bear the Ark of God, I have learned about this secret plot:

"Achitophel advised Absalom to let him choose twelve thousand fighting men, and he would come on and attack David in the night while he was unaware and was weary with his violent toil.

"But I advised Absalom to get a greater army and gather men from Dan to Bersabe to come upon him strongly in the fields.

"Now send your sons Ahimaas and Jonathan to deliver these secrets to the king. Let them advise him not to stay this night out in the open field, but to get over the Jordan River immediately, lest he and all his people kiss the sword and die."

Sadoc said, "Go, Ahimaas and Jonathan, and immediately convey this message to King David."

Ahimaas replied, "Father, we will, if Absalom's chief spies don't stop us and keep us here."

CHAPTER 13

— Scene 12 —

Semei stood on a road near the village of Bahurim, which was located east of the Mount of Olives. Semei had been a follower of Saul, and he hated David because David had succeeded Saul as King of Israel. He regarded David, who had been a shepherd in his youth, as a tyrant. His pockets were filled with stones to throw as weapons, and he was waiting for David.

Semei said to himself, "The man of Israel who has ruled as king, or rather as the tyrant of the land, bolstering his hateful head upon the throne that God unworthily has blessed him with, shall now, I hope, lay as low as Hell, and be deposed from his detested chair — the throne he sits on.

"Oh, I wish that my bosom could by nature bear a sea of poison that would be poured upon David's cursed head — the head that sacred balm has graced and consecrated King of Israel!

"Or I wish that my breath were made the smoke of Hell, infected with the sighs of damned souls, or with the reeking vapor of the throat of that serpent that feeds on adders, toads, and venomous roots, so that, as I opened my revenging lips to curse the shepherd for his tyranny, my words might cast rank poison into his pores, and make his swollen and rankling sinews crack like the combat-blows that break the clouds when Jove's brave champions — God's angels — fight with fiery swords."

King David and his men were traveling east.

Seeing David, Semei said to himself, "See where is coming he whom my soul abhors! I have prepared my pocket full of stones, mingled with earth and dust, to throw at him, Bursting with disdain, I greet him with stones and earth and dust."

King David, Joab, Abisai, Ithay, and others arrived on the scene.

Semei yelled, "Come forth, thou murderer and wicked man. The lord has brought upon thy cursed head the guiltless, innocent blood of Saul and all his sons, whose royal throne thy baseness has usurped.

"And, to revenge it deeply on thy soul, the Lord has given the kingdom to thy son Absalom, and he shall avenge the traitorous wrongs of Saul."

Apparently, Semei meant that Absalom would avenge the traitorous wrongs committed against Saul. Or perhaps Saul had committed a wrong: the wrong of acting in such a way that allowed David to become king.

Semei continued:

"Even as thy sin has still importuned Heaven, so shall thy murders and adultery be punished in the sight of Israel, as thou deserve, with blood, with death, and with Hell.

"Hence, murderer, flee away from here!

"Let me alone to take away his head."

He threw stones and earth and dust at David.

Abisai, who was the son of Zeruia, asked about Semei, "Why does this dead dog curse my lord the king?"

King David said, "Why meddles thus the son of Zeruia to interrupt the action of our God?

"Semei accosts me with this reproach because the Lord has sent him to reprove the sins of David, printed in David's own brows with blood. David blushes for his conscience's guilt.

"Who dares, then, ask him why he curses me?"

Hearing David, Semei said, "If, then, thy conscience tells thee that thou have sinned, and that thy life is odious to the world, command thy followers to shun thy face; and by thyself here make away thy soul and commit suicide, so that I may stand and glory in thy shame."

David replied, "I am not desperate, Semei, like thyself, for I instead trust the covenant of my God, which is founded on mercy, built with repentance, and finished with the glory of my soul."

David knew that he had sinned, but he was hopeful and not desperate about his future life.

Semei said, "You are a murderer — and you hope for mercy in thy end! May hate and destruction sit upon thy brows to watch the exit from your body of thy damned ghost, which with thy last gasp they'll take and tear, hurling a piece in every part of Hell. Hence, murderer, thou shame to Israel, foul lecher, drunkard, plague to Heaven and earth!"

He again threw stones and earth and dust at King David.

Joab said, "Does David think it is merciful to refrain like this from following the laws of self-preservation in this extremity of his distress, in order to allow his subjects to be so reckless in words and deeds?

"Send hence the dog with sorrow to his grave."

Joab and Abisai, his brother — both were sons of Zeruia — wanted Semei dead.

King David said, "Why should the sons of Zeruia seek to check Semei's spirit, which the Lord has thus inspired?

"Behold, my son Absalom, who issued from my flesh, seeks to take my life with equal fury to that which thou two want to take the life of Semei.

"How much more then the grandson of Jemini — Semei — wants to take my life, chiefly since Semei does nothing but God's command?

"It may happen that God will look on me this day with gracious eyes, and as a result of Semei's cursing bless the heart of David in his bitterness."

Semei said, "Do thou fret and vex my soul with sufferance and tolerance? Oh, I wish that the souls of Isboseth and Abner, whom thou sent swimming to their graves in blood, with wounds freshly bleeding, gasping for revenge, were here to execute my burning hate!"

Isboseth was Saul's son, and Abner was the commander of Isboseth's army. The two men quarreled when Isboseth took one of Abner's concubines. Abner left Isboseth and attempted to join the side of David, but Joab killed him because Abner had earlier killed Joab's brother. Isboseth's own soldiers killed Isboseth.

Semei continued, "But I will hunt thy foot with curses still.

"Hence, monster, murderer, mirror of contempt!"

He again threw stones and earth and dust at King David.

Ahimaas and Jonathan entered the scene, bearing Cusay's news for King David.

Ahimaas said, "Long life to David, and death to his enemies!"

"Welcome, Ahimaas and Jonathan," King David said. "What news does Cusay send to thy lord the king?"

Ahimaas said, "Cusay wishes my lord the king to cross the Jordan River immediately, lest he and all his people perish here, for wise Achitophel has counseled Absalom to take advantage of your weary arms, and come this night upon you in the fields and attack you.

"But the Lord has made Achitophel's counsel scorned, and Cusay's policy preferred with praise. Cusay's policy was to enroll every Israelite man as a soldier, and so attack you in their pride of strength, vastly outnumbering you and your men."

Referring to King David in the third person, Jonathan said, "Abiathar in addition entreats the king to send his men of war against his son Absalom, and not risk his person in the field."

Abiathar did not want King David to fight in the forthcoming battle.

King David said, "Thanks to Abiathar, and to you both, and to my Cusay, whom the Lord reward. But ten times treble — ten times three — thanks to His soft hand Whose pleasant touch has made my heart to dance, and play and sing Him praises in my zealous breast, who turned the counsel of Achitophel into accordance with the prayers of his servant's — my — lips.

"Now we will cross the river all this night, and in the morning we will sound the voice of war, the voice of bloody and unkindly and un-kin-ly war of son against father."

Joab said, "Tell us how thou will divide thy men, and who shall have the special charge herein."

He was asking into how many battalions King David would divide the soldiers, and who would lead each battalion.

King David said, "Joab, thou thyself shall for thy charge conduct the first of three battalions of all my valiant men.

"Abisai's valor shall lead the second of three battalions.

"The third of three battalions fair Ithay, whom I most should grace for the comfort he has done to David's woes, shall lead.

"And I myself will follow with my guard in the midst."

Ithay said, "That David should not do; for if we soldiers were to flee from battle, even ten thousand of us would not be valued half as much by David's enemies as he himself is. Thy soldiers, loving thee, deny thee this. Thy soldiers won't let thee participate in the battle."

Ithay was saying that if King David's soldiers were to be forced to flee from the battlefield, David's enemies would devote all their efforts to finding and killing David, even if it meant missing the opportunity to kill ten thousand of David's soldiers. For that reason, King David's soldiers wanted King David to not participate in the battle.

King David said, "What seems best to them, my people, then, that will David do.

"But now, my lords and captains, hear the voice of him — me — who never yet pierced piteous Heaven with his prayers in vain. So then let my words not slip lightly through your ears.

"For my sake, spare the young man Absalom. Joab, thyself did once use friendly words to reconcile my incensed heart to him. If, then, thy love to thy kinsman is sound and unimpaired, and thou will prove thyself to be a perfect Israelite, befriend him with deeds, and touch not a hair of his — touch not that fair hair with which the wanton, playful winds delight to play, and love to make curl, and in which the nightingales would build their nests, and make sweet bowers in every golden tress to sing their lover to sleep every night.

"Oh, Joab, don't spoil Jove's — God's — fair ornaments, which he has sent to solace David's soul!

"The best, you see, my lords, are swift to sin. When we sin, our feet are washed with the milk of roe deer, and dried again with coals of lightning. We enjoy committing the sin, but we hate enduring the punishment of that sin.

"Oh, Lord, thou see the proudest sin's poor slave, and with his bridle thou pull him to the grave!

"For my sake, then, spare lovely Absalom."

Ithay replied, "We will, my lord, for thy sake favor him. We will spare Absalom."

CHAPTER 14

— Scene 13 —

In his house, Achitophel stood alone, holding a noose.

He said to himself, "Now Achitophel has set his house in order and settled his affairs and taken leave of every pleasure there."

Looking at the noose, he said, "On this depends Achitophel's 'delights,' and in this circle must his life be closed."

He paused and then continued, "The wise Achitophel, whose counsel proved always as sound for fortunate success as if men asked the oracle of God, is now treated like the fool of Israel.

"So then set thy angry soul upon thy soul's wings, and let her fly into the shadow of death; and for my death let Heaven forever weep, making huge floods with its tears upon the land I leave, to ravish them and all their fairest fruits. Let the flood of tears destroy the agricultural crops of Israel. Let all the sighs I breathed for this disgrace hang on my hedges like eternal mists, to serve as mourning garments for their master's death."

Garments were sometimes hung on hedges to dry after being washed.

Achitophel continued, "Open, earth, and take thy miserable son into the bowels of thy cursed womb. Once in a surfeit thou did spew him forth. Now because of deadly hunger suck him in again, and let his body be poison to thy veins."

The earth had once over-eaten and then vomited forth Achitophel; now, he wanted the earth to devour him.

He continued, "And now, thou Hellish instrument of Heaven, at once execute the arrest of Jove's just decision, and stop the breast of him who curses Israel."

Jove literally refers to Jupiter, the Roman name of the king of the gods, but metaphorically it refers to God. All of God's decisions are just, and God had decided to have Achitophel treated like a fool. To stop being treated like a fool and thereby arrest Jove's just decision, Achitophel committed suicide.

The suicide stopped the heart of Achitophel, who had just now cursed Israel: "... and for my death let Heaven forever weep, making huge floods with its tears upon the land I leave, to ravish them and all their fairest fruits. Let the flood of tears destroy the agricultural crops of Israel."

2 Samuel 17:23 states, *"And when Ahithophel saw that his counsel was not followed, he saddled his ass, and arose and gat him home to his own house, and to his own city, and put his household in order, and hanged himself, and died, and was buried in the sepulcher of his father"* (1568 Bishop's Bible).

CHAPTER 15

In the Wood of Ephraim, Absalom stood with Amasa and the rest of his train.

Absalom had gathered many soldiers and was ready to fight King David's army.

The battle was about to start.

Absalom said, "Now for the crown and throne of Israel to be confirmed with the power of my sword and written with David's blood upon the blade.

"Now, Jove, let forth the golden firmament — the stars — to look on him — me — with all Thy fiery eyes that Thou have made to give their glories light.

"To show Thou love the power of me, who is Thy hand, let fall a wreath of stars upon my head, whose influence may govern Israel with state exceeding all her other kings.

"Fight, lords and captains, so that your sovereign's face may shine in honor brighter than the sun; and with the virtue of my beauteous rays make this fair land as fruitful as the fields that with sweet milk and honey overflowed. God, in the whizzing of a pleasant wind, shall march upon the tops of mulberry-trees, to cool all breasts that burn with any griefs, as in the past when he was good to Moses' men.

"By day the Lord shall sit within a cloud, to guide your footsteps to the fields of joy, and in the night a pillar, bright as fire, shall go before you, like a second sun, in which is the essence of his godhead.

"So that day and night you may be brought to peace, and never swerve from that delightsome path that leads your souls to perfect happiness, this shall God do for joy when I am king.

"So then fight, brave captains, so that these joys may fly into your bosoms with sweet victory."

CHAPTER 16

— **Scene 15** —

The battle, which had taken place by the Wood of Ephraim, was over. Absalom's army had lost, and he had attempted to escape by riding away on a mule. But his long hair got caught in the branches of a tree, the mule kept going, and Absalom was left hanging by his hair.

Absalom said to himself, "What angry angel, sitting in these shadows, has laid his cruel hands upon my hair and holds my body thus between Heaven and earth?

"Has Absalom no soldier near his hand who may untwine for me this unpleasant curl, or wound and cut this tree that seizes his lord?"

One of his soldiers could untangle and release his hair or cut off the branches that held Absalom's hair.

Absalom did not mention cutting his hair in order to be released.

"Oh, God, see the glory of Thy hand, and the choicest fruit of nature's workmanship, hang, like a rotten branch, upon this tree, fit for the axe and ready for the fire!

"Since thou withhold all ordinary help to release my body from this bond of death, oh, let my beauty fill these senseless plants with the sense and power to release me from this plague, and work some wonder to prevent the death of Absalom, whose life thou made a special miracle!"

Joab and one of his soldiers entered the scene.

The soldier said to Joab, "My lord, I saw the young Prince Absalom hanging by the hair upon a shady oak, and he could by no means get himself freed."

Joab asked, "Why didn't thou slay the wicked Absalom, that rebel to his father and to Heaven, so that I might have given thee for thy pains ten silver shekels and a golden belt?"

The soldier replied, "Not for a thousand shekels would I slay the son of King David. Absalom's father ordered that neither thou, nor Abisai, nor the son of Gath — Ithay — should touch Absalom with the

70

stroke of deadly violence. King David's order was given in the hearing of us all, and, if I had done it, then, I know, thou thyself, before thou would abide and suffer the king's rebuke, would have accused me as a man of death. I would have been executed immediately."

Joab said, "I must not now stand trifling here with thee."

As a military man, Joab knew that some rebels, despite being pardoned, rebel again.

Absalom begged, "Help, Joab, help, oh, help thy Absalom! Let not thy angry thoughts be laid in blood, in the blood of him who in former times cherished and nourished thee, and softened thy sweet heart with friendly love.

"Oh, give me once again my father's sight, my dearest father and my princely sovereign, so that, as I shed tears of blood from my wounded heart before his face, the ground may witness, and the heavens record, my last submission perfect and full of pity."

Joab replied, "Rebel to nature, hate to Heaven and earth! Shall I give help to him who thirsts after the soul of his dear father and my sovereign lord? Now see, the Lord has tangled in a tree the health and glory of thy stubborn heart, and made thy pride curbed with a plant that lacks the senses of an animal.

"Now, Absalom, how does the Lord regard the beauty whereupon thy hope was built, and which thou thought God's grace did glory in?

"Don't thou find now, with fear of instant death, that God does not love any superficially handsome body or superficially handsome face, when the valuable soul, which ought to be virtuous, is stuffed with nothing but pride and stubbornness?

"But I am preaching to thee while I should revenge thy cursed sin that stained Israel and makes her fields blush with her children's blood!

"Take that as part of thy deserved plague, which worthily no torment can inflict. You deserve to be punished so much more than this."

Joab stabbed Absalom with a spear.

Absalom cried, "Oh, Joab, Joab, cruel, ruthless Joab! Herewith thou wound thy kingly sovereign's — David's — heart, whose heavenly temper hates the sight of his children's blood, and who will be sick, I know, for Absalom."

He addressed his absent father: "Oh, my dear father, I wish that thy melting eyes might pierce this thicket to behold thy son, thy dearest son, gored with a mortal spear!"

He then said, "Yet, Joab, pity me. Pity my father, Joab. Pity the distress of the soul of him who mourns my life, and who will die, I know, when he hears of my death."

Joab said, "If he were so compassionate about thy condition, why did he send me against thee with the sword? All Joab intends to do to give thee pleasure is to dispatch and kill thee quickly and thus stop thy pain.

"Absalom, believe that Joab's pity is in this; in this, proud Absalom, is Joab's love for thee."

Joab stabbed Absalom again and then exited with the soldier.

Absalom said, "Such love, such pity may Israel's God send thee, Joab, and for His — God's — love to David pity me!"

He again addressed his absent father: "Ah, my dear father, see thy bowels bleed. See death assault thy dearest Absalom. See, pity, pardon, pray for Absalom!"

Five or six soldiers who were enemies to Absalom entered the scene.

The first soldier said, "See where the rebel in his glory hangs.

"Where is the virtue — the power — of thy beauty, Absalom? Will any of us here now fear thy looks, or be in love with thy golden hair wherein was wrapped rebellion against thy sire, and ropes prepared to stop thy father's breath?"

The image was of Absalom intending to strangle his father with his — Absalom's — long hair.

"Our captain Joab has begun to pledge a drink to us, and here's an end to thee and all thy sins."

By wounding Absalom, it was as if Joab had began to drink a toast to his soldiers' health. With Absalom dead, the rebellion would be over, and King David's soldiers would no longer die in the battles of civil war.

The soldiers stabbed Absalom, who died.

The first soldier said, "Come, let us take the beautiful rebel down, and in some ditch in the midst of this dark wood, let us bury his body beneath a heap of stones. Let us bury the body of him whose stony heart did hunt his father's death."

Joab, Abisai, and some soldiers, including a drummer and an ensign carrying the army's flag, entered the scene.

Joab said, "Well done, brave soldiers! Take the traitor down, and in this miry ditch inter his bones, covering his hateful breast with heaps of stones. This shady thicket of the dark wood of Ephraim shall always and forever scowl on his cursed grave. Night-ravens and owls shall ring his fatal knell and sit exclaiming on his damned soul. There shall they heap their preys of carrion, until all his grave shall be clad with stinking bones, so that the grave may make the senses of every man loathe the sight and stink of his grave.

"So shall his end breed horror to his reputation, and eternal shame to his traitorous deed."

CHAPTER 17

— Chorus 2 —

The Chorus said this:

"Oh, dread-causing President — God — of His just judgment, Whose holy heart is never touched with compassion solely for fickle beauty or for glorious shapes, but is touched with compassion for the virtue of an upright soul that is humble and zealous in his inward thoughts, although in his face and body he is loathsome and deformed!

"Now, since this story lends us enough abundance to make a third discourse of David's life, adding thereto his most renowned death, and all the deaths of all those whom at his death he judged, here end we this section, and what here is lacking to please the audience, we will supply with treble willingness."

Note:

Actually, King David's death does not appear in the play or in this retelling of the play.

CHAPTER 18

Near the battlefield, trumpets sounded. Joab, Ahimaas, and Cusay marched onto the scene. With them were Amasa and all the other followers of Absalom. Amasa was King David's nephew, but he had been the leader of Absalom's army.

Joab said, "Soldiers of Israel, and you sons of Judah, who have fought in these painful and disgusting battles, and ripped old Israel's bowels with your swords, the godless general of your stubborn arms — Absalom — has been brought by Israel's helper — God — to the grave: a grave of shame, and the scorn of all the tribes of Israel.

"Now, then, to save your honors from the dust, and keep your hot bloods at a moderate temper by your bones, let Joab's ensign shelter your manly heads. Direct your eyes, your weapons, and your hearts to guard the life of David from his foes. Error has masked your much-too-forward minds, and you have sinned against the king chosen by God to rule Israel, against his life, for whom your lives are blessed, and you have followed a usurper to the battlefield.

"In that usurper's just death, your deaths are threatened.

"But Joab pities your disordered and confused souls, and therefore he offers pardon, peace, and love to all who will be friendly and reconciled to Israel's welfare, to David, and to Heaven."

Joab wanted Absalom's former followers to again become faithful followers of King David.

Joab then said, "Amasa, thou are the leader of the army that under Absalom have raised their arms. Now be a captain wise and politic, careful and loving for thy soldiers' lives, and lead them to this honorable league of friendship."

If Amasa, the leader of Absalom's army, were to pledge his loyalty to King David, the defeated rebel soldiers were likely to do the same.

"I will," Amasa said. "At least, I'll do my best. And for the gracious offer thou have made I give thee thanks, as much as I give thee thanks for allowing me to keep my head."

Amasa, who could have been beheaded as punishment for being a traitor, then said to his defeated soldiers, "So then, you deceived poor souls of Israel, since now you see the errors you fell into, now be appeased with thanks and due submission, and as you see my — your captain's — precedent, here cast we, then, our swords at Joab's feet, submitting with all zeal and reverence our goods and bodies to his gracious hands."

Amasa and his defeated soldiers cast down their swords and knelt.

Joab said, "Stand up, and all of you take your swords again."

All stood up and took their swords.

Joab continued, "David and Joab shall be blessed herein."

Ahimaas, the son of the high priest Sadoc, said, "Now let me go inform my lord the king about how God has freed him from his enemies."

"Another time, Ahimaas, not now," Joab said. "But, Cusay, go thyself, and tell the king the happy message of our good success."

"I will, my lord," Cusay replied, "and I thank thee for thy grace."

He exited.

Ahimaas asked, "What if thy servant — me — should go, too, my lord?"

Joab asked, "What news have thou to bring since Cusay has gone?"

Ahimaas had no new news, but he could go by a route different from the one Cusay took and perhaps get to King David faster than Cusay could.

Ahimaas requested, "Yet give Ahimaas the contentment he would receive by running on so sweet a charge."

Much of the message was sweet: The army opposing King David had been decisively defeated and the civil war was over. But part of the message was not sweet: Absalom, King David's rebelling son, was dead.

Joab replied, "Run, if thou will, and may peace be with thy steps."

Ahimaas exited.

Joab ordered Amasa and the defeated soldiers, "Now follow, so that you may salute the king with humble hearts and reconciled souls."

Amasa said, "We follow, Joab, and go to our gracious king, and our swords shall honor him to our deaths."

CHAPTER 19

— Scene 17 —

King David, Bathsheba, Solomon, Chileab, Adonia, and Nathan the prophet were at David's headquarters at Manahaim. With them were their trains of attendants.

Solomon, Chileab, and Adonia were three of David's sons. Solomon's mother was Bathsheba.

None knew yet that King David's army had conquered the rebels and that Absalom was dead.

Bathsheba asked her husband, King David, "Why does my lord, the lamp of Israel, from whose bright eyes all eyes receive their light, dim the glory of his sweet face, and paint his countenance with his heart's distress?"

King David's face showed his distress. He was worried about the battle, and he was worried about his son Absalom.

Bathsheba continued, "Why should his thoughts retain a sadness, when every pleasure kneels before his throne, and sues for sweet acceptance with his grace?"

As king, David had many pleasures available to him. Why, then, should he be sad?

Bathsheba continued, "Just take up your lute, and make the mountains dance, recall the sphere of the sun, and restrain the clouds, give ears to trees, make savage lions tame, impose still silence on the loudest winds, and fill the fairest day with foulest storms."

King David was skilled with the harp, and Bathsheba attributed to his skill such powers as making good weather bad, and bad weather good.

She continued, "Then why should passions of much meaner power bear head against the heart of Israel?"

King David — the heart of Israel — was allowing the emotion of melancholy to affect him.

King David replied, "Fair Bathsheba, thou might increase the strength of these thy arguments, drawn from my skill, by urging thy sweet sight to my sad mood. Your beauty has always served as sacred balm past all earthly joys to cheer me up and make me forget my griefs.

"But, Bathsheba, fair Peace is the daughter of the Highest and her beauty builds the towers of Israel. Fair Peace is she who in chains of pearl and unicorn horn leads in her wake the ancient golden world, the world that Adam held in paradise, whose breath refines all infectious airs, and makes the meadows smile at her arrival ... she, she ... my dearest Bathsheba, by 'she' I mean fair Peace, the goddess of our graces here ... has fled the streets of fair Jerusalem, the fields of Israel, and the heart of David, leading my comforts in her golden chains linked to the life and soul of Absalom."

King David was mourning because Israel was not at peace and fair Peace had departed, taking with her the things that would comfort him. Among the things that would comfort him were the life and soul of his son Absalom.

Bathsheba said, "Then is the pleasure of my sovereign's heart so wrapped within the bosom of that son Absalom that the result is that Solomon, whom Israel's God affects and to whom you gave the name 'Solomon' because of God's love, should be no salve to comfort David's soul?"

Bathsheba gave birth to her second son with David after God had forgiven David's sins; because of God's forgiveness, David named his son Solomon, a name that means Peace.

2 Samuel 12:24 states that King David *"called his name Solomon, and the Lord loved him"* (1568 Bishop's Bible).

King David said, "Solomon, my love, is David's lord. Our God has named him lord of Israel. In him — for that, and since he is thy son — David must necessarily be pleased at the heart, and he shall surely sit upon my throne."

Solomon was figuratively David's lord because Solomon would succeed him as King of Israel.

King David continued, "But Absalom, the beauty of my bones, fair Absalom, the portrait of love, sweet Absalom, the image of content, must claim a portion in his father's care, and be in life and death King David's son."

Nathan the prophet said, "Yet, as my lord has said, let Solomon reign, whom God in naming has anointed king.

"Now is he apt to learn the eternal laws, whose knowledge being rooted in his youth will beautify his age with glorious fruits."

Solomon was still young, and he could learn knowledge that would take root in him now and lead to fruits for Israel later when he ruled.

Nathan the prophet continued, "In contrast, Absalom, incensed with graceless pride, usurps and stains the kingdom with his sin.

"Let Solomon be made thy staff of age, fair Israel's rest, and the honor of thy race."

King David said, "Tell me, my Solomon, will thou embrace thy father's moral instructions and engrave them in thy heart, and satisfy my zealous desire for thy renown with the practice of such sacred principles as shall concern the state of Israel?"

King David wanted Solomon to rule well and acquire a lasting reputation as a righteous king.

Solomon replied, "My royal father, if the heavenly zeal, which for my welfare feeds upon your soul, were not sustained with the virtue of my own, and if the sweet accents of your cheerful voice should not each hour reach my ears as sweetly as the breath of Heaven reaches him who gasps while being scorched with the summer's sun, I should be guilty of unpardoned sin, fearing the plague of Heaven and the shame of earth.

"But since I myself vow to learn the skill and holy secrets of his — God's — mighty hand whose cunning tunes the music of my soul, it would content me, father, first to learn these things:

"How the Eternal framed the firmament."

Solomon wanted to know how God created the heavens.

He continued, "Which bodies lead their influence by fire, and which are filled with hoary winter's ice."

Astrologers believed that heavenly bodies influenced human lives. The fiery heavenly bodies are stars, which can have a beneficial or malicious influence. The icy heavenly bodies are comets, whose appearance in the sky was regarded as portending evil.

Solomon continued, "What sign is rainy, and what star is fair."

The constellation Orion appeared in late autumn when bad weather appeared. Astronomers have long used the stars to make weather predictions.

The three astrological water signs are Cancer, Scorpio, and Pisces. The three astrological fire signs are Aries, Leo, and Sagittarius. The three astrological earth signs are Taurus, Virgo, and Capricorn. The three astrological air signs are Gemini, Libra, and Aquarius.

Solomon continued, "Why by the rules of true proportion the year is still divided into months, the months to days, and the days to certain hours."

The phrase "true proportion" means "proper ratio."

We must pay attention to astronomy today to keep our calendars up to date. The Earth orbits the Sun once every 365 days, 5 hours, 48 minutes, and 45 seconds, and so every four years we have a leap year in which one extra day is added to the calendar.

Understanding astronomy involves understanding God's creation that is the universe.

Solomon continued, "What fruitful race shall fill the future world, and for what time shall this round building — the Earth — stand."

Today, we also want to know about the future of humanity and the planet Earth.

Solomon continued, "What magistrates, what kings shall keep in awe men's minds with bridles of the eternal law."

The first things Solomon mentioned were mainly theoretical knowledge, but this was practical knowledge. Studying good and effective kings can help people learn how to rule well and effectively.

King David advised, "Wade not too far, my boy, in waves too deep. The feeble eyes of our aspiring thoughts behold present things and record past things. But things to come exceed our human reach, and they are not depicted yet in angels' eyes. For those things to come, submit thy sense, and say these things:

"*Oh, Lord, Who now is creating the future world, Thou know all to come not by the course of heavenly stars, comets, and planets, not by frail conjectures of inferior signs, not by monstrous floods, not by flights and flocks of birds, not by the bowels of a sacrificed beast, and not by the figures of some hidden art, but by a true and natural presage, laying the ground and perfect architecture of all our actions now before Thine eyes, from Adam to the end of Adam's seed — the last man on earth.*"

The inferior — worthless — signs can include astrological signs. Such unusual natural happenings as huge floods were sometimes thought to predict bad things in the human and political world. Some people thought that the flight of birds — either to the lucky or the unlucky side — could predict the course of future events. Priests examined the entrails of sacrificed animals in an attempt to understand the future. Some people used occult symbols such as those on Tarot cards to try to correctly predict the future. All of these ways to try to predict the future are superstitions.

A true and natural presage is a true and natural sign of what will occur. Today, we make predictions based on science, which is based on knowledge of natural laws and mathematics.

King David continued, "*Oh, Heaven, protect my weakness with thy strength! Look on me so that I may view thy face, and see these secrets written in thy brows.*

"*Oh, sun, come shoot thy rays upon my moon! So that now my eyes, eclipsed to the earth, may brightly be refined and cleared and so shine to Heaven.*

"*Transform me from this flesh, so that I may live, before my death, spiritually reborn with thee.*

"*Oh, Thou great God, ravish my earthly spirit!*

"*Do these things so that for the time a more-than-human skill may feed the organons — bodily instruments — of all my mind.*

"*Do these things so that when I think, Thy thoughts may be my guide, and, when I speak, I may be made by choice the perfect echo of Thy heavenly voice.*"

King David paused and then said, "Thus say, my son, and thou shall learn them all."

Solomon said, "A secret inspired frenzy enraptures my soul, lifting my mind above her human bounds, and, just as the eagle, flying from her resting place with violent hunger, towering in the air, seizes her feathered prey, and thinks to eat, but seeing then a cloud beneath her feet, lets the fowl fall, and is emboldened with eyes intending to challenge and defy the sun, and soars close to the sun's stately sphere, so Solomon, mounted on the burning wings of divine zeal, lets fall his mortal food, and cheers his senses with celestial air, walks in the golden starry labyrinth, and holds his eyes fixed on Jehovah's forehead."

Eagles were thought to be able to look directly at the sun; Solomon wanted to be able to look directly at God.

Solomon continued, "Good father, teach me further what to do."

Nathan the prophet said, "See, David, how his aspiring spirit mounts and is even now of a height to wear a crown. So then make him the promise that he may succeed you as King of Israel, and make old Israel's bones rest from the turmoil of war."

King David said, "Nathan, thou prophet, whose ancestor was Jesse, from whom the Messiah shall be descended, I promise thee and lovely Bathsheba that my Solomon shall govern after me."

Bathsheba said, "May He — God — who has touched thee with this righteous thought preserve the harbor of thy thoughts in peace!"

A messenger arrived and said, "My lord, thy servants of the watch-guard have seen one running here from the wars."

King David said, "If he has come alone, he is bringing news."

The messenger added, "Another man has thy servant seen, my lord, whose style of running much resembles that of Sadoc's son."

"He is a good man and brings good tidings," King David said.

Ahimaas, the son of Sadoc, entered the scene and said, "May peace and contentment be with my lord the king, whom Israel's God has blessed with victory."

King David asked about the other matter that he was greatly concerned about, "Tell me, Ahimaas, does my Absalom still live?"

Ahimaas answered, "I saw a troop of soldiers gathered, but I don't know what the tumult might mean."

Ahimaas knew that Absalom was dead, but he also knew that telling a king bad news can be dangerous.

King David said, "Stand nearby, until some other messenger may inform the heart of David with a happy truth."

Cusay entered the scene and said, "May happiness and honor live with David's soul, whom God has blessed with the conquest of his foes."

King David asked, "But, Cusay, does the young man Absalom still live?"

Cusay replied, "May the stubborn enemies to David's peace, and all who cast their spears against his crown, fare always like the young man Absalom! For as he rode through the woods of Ephraim, which fought for thee as much as all thy men, his hair was tangled in a shady oak, and hanging there, he sustained the stroke of well-deserved death by Joab and his men."

Many of the enemy soldiers, in addition to Absalom, had died in the woods of Ephraim.

"Has Absalom sustained the stroke of death?" King David said. "Die, David, because of the death of Absalom, and make this cursed news the bloody spears that through Absalom's bowels rip thy wretched breast.

"Hence, David, walk the solitary woods, and in the shade of some cedar that the thunder slew, and fire from Heaven — lightning — made its branches black, sit and mourn the decease of Absalom.

"Against the body of that lightning-blasted plant, break thy ivory lute into a thousand slivers and hang thy stringless harp upon the dead cedar's boughs, and through the sapless hollow-sounding trunk bellow the torments that perplex thy soul.

"There let the winds sit sighing until they burst. Let a tempest, muffled with a pitch-dark cloud, threaten the forests with her hellish face, and, mounted fiercely on her iron wings, tear up by the roots the wretched engine of destruction — the tree — that held my dearest Absalom, leading to his death.

"Then let them toss my broken lute to Heaven, even to His — God's — hands that whip me with the strings, to show how sadly His poor shepherd sings."

He went into his pavilion — a large tent — and sat alone with his back to the others.

Bathsheba said, "Die, Bathsheba, to see thy David mourn, to hear his tunes of anguish and of Hell.

"Oh, help, my David, help thy Bathsheba" — she knelt and then lay prostrate — "whose heart is pierced with thy breathy swords, and bursts with the burden of ten thousand griefs!"

King David's cries as he mourned the death of Absalom were swords made out of breath that pierced Bathsheba's heart.

Bathsheba continued speaking about King David's sorrows, "Now thy sorrows sit and suck my blood. Oh, I wish that my blood might be poison to the powers of thy sorrows, and I wish that their lips might draw my bosom dry, as long as David's love might ease him, though she — I, Bathsheba — die!"

Nathan the prophet criticized the extreme grief of David and Bathsheba: "These violent passions don't come from above; they don't come from Heaven. David and Bathsheba offend God the Highest by mourning in this immeasurable way."

King David stood and looked out of his pavilion and said, "Oh, Absalom, Absalom! Oh, my son, my son! I wish to God that I had died for Absalom! But he is dead! Ah, dead! Absalom is dead. And David lives to die for Absalom."

King David sat again inside the pavilion and mourned.

Joab, Abisai, Ithay, and their train of soldiers arrived.

Joab asked, "Why does the queen lie so prostrate on the ground? Why is this company so sadly faced? Why is the king now absent from his soldiers, and why isn't he marching in triumph through the gates?"

He drew back part of the pavilion, revealing King David inside, and said to him:

"David, awake. If sleep has shut thine eyes — the sleep of affection — and so thou cannot see the honor offered to the victor's head, then know Joab brings conquest pierced on his spear, and joy from all the tribes of Israel."

David's affection for the dead Absalom was making him not rejoice in his country's military victory. It was deadening him to the pleasure he would normally have felt because of this good news.

King David asked, "Thou man of blood, thou sepulcher of death, whose marble breast entombs my bowels alive, didn't I order thee, indeed, beg thee, even for my sake, to spare my Absalom?

"And have thou now, out of scorn for what would contribute to David's health, and out of scorn for doing my heart some happiness, given him the sword and spilt his purple soul?"

This society used the word "purple" to refer to both royalty and the color of blood.

Joab, a military man who rejoiced in the victory and knew that it would greatly help Israel, said:

"Does it irritate David that he breathes as a victor and that Judah and the battlefields of Israel should clean their faces and remove from their faces their children's blood?

"Are thou weary of thy royal rule?

"Is Israel's throne a serpent in thine eyes?

"Is He — God — Who set thee there so far from and undeserving of thanks, that thou must curse His servant — me — for His sake?

"Have thou not said that, as is the morning light of the cloudless morning, so should be thine house?"

"Have thou not said that your house should not be as flowers that by the brightest rain grow up quickly and as quickly fade?"

"Have thou not said that the wicked are as thorns, which cannot be preserved and protected with the hand, and that the man who shall touch them must be armed with coats of iron and garments made of steel, and with the shaft of a protected spear?"

Harmful thorns ought not to be protected; they ought to be destroyed.

Joab then said, "And are thou angry that the life is now cut off of the man who led the guiltless swarming to their deaths, and was more wicked than an army of men?

"Advance thee from thy melancholy den! Come out of thy pavilion! And deck thy body with thy blissful robes, or, by the Lord Who sways the Heaven I swear that I'll lead thine armies to another king who shall cheer them for their princely chivalry, and not sit daunted, frowning in the dark, at a time when his fair looks, refreshed with oil and wine, should dart gladdening beams into their bosoms, and fill their stomachs with triumphant feasts.

"If thou act the way the other king acts, then when elsewhere stern War shall sound his trumpet, and call another army to the battlefield, Reputation still may bring thy valiant soldiers home after their victory, and for their service Reputation may happily confess that she lacked enough worthy trumpets to sound their prowess. Their prowess was so great that she needed additional trumpets.

"You have a choice to make.

"Take thou this course I am recommending and live. Come out of thy pavilion and reward thy troops and lead Israel and ensure that your reputation will live.

"Or refuse to take this course I am recommending, stay in your pavilion, mourn as I lead away your soldiers, and allow your reputation to die."

Abisai said, "Come, brother, let him sit there until he sinks. Some other king shall advance the name of Joab."

The brothers Joab and Abisai started to leave.

Bathsheba rose and said, "Oh, wait, my lords, stay! David mourns no more, but rises to give honor to your acts."

King David came out of the pavilion and said about Absalom, "Then happy are thou, David's fairest son, who, freed from the yoke of earthly toils, and sequestered from any perception of human sins, thy soul shall enjoy the sacred lodging — Paradise — of those divine ideas that present thy changed spirit with a Heaven of bliss.

"Then thou are gone; ah, thou are gone, my son! To Heaven, I hope, my Absalom has gone. Thy soul there placed in honor of the saints, or angels clad with immortality, shall reap a sevenfold grace for all thy griefs.

"Thy eyes, now no longer eyes but shining stars, shall deck the flaming heavens with novel lamps.

"There thou shall taste the drink of seraphim, and cheer thy feelings with the food of archangels.

"Thy day of rest, thy holy Sabbath day, shall be eternal; and, with the curtain drawn back, thou shall behold thy Sovereign face to face with wonder, knit in triple unity, unity infinite and innumerable."

He then said to Joab and Abisai, "Courage, brave captains! Joab's tale has stirred me, and made the suit of Israel preferred. I now will rule Israel to the best of my abilities. Now may old Israel and his daughters sing."

Joab said, "Bravely resolved, and spoken like a king."

APPENDIX A: ABOUT THE AUTHOR

It was a dark and stormy night. Suddenly a cry rang out, and on a hot summer night in 1954, Josephine, wife of Carl Bruce, gave birth to a boy — me. Unfortunately, this young married couple allowed Reuben Saturday, Josephine's brother, to name their first-born. Reuben, aka "The Joker," decided that Bruce was a nice name, so he decided to name me Bruce Bruce. I have gone by my middle name — David — ever since.

Being named Bruce David Bruce hasn't been all bad. Bank tellers remember me very quickly, so I don't often have to show an ID. It can be fun in charades, also. When I was a counselor as a teenager at Camp Echoing Hills in Warsaw, Ohio, a fellow counselor gave the signs for "sounds like" and "two words," then she pointed to a bruise on her leg twice. Bruise Bruise? Oh yeah, Bruce Bruce is the answer!

Uncle Reuben, by the way, gave me a haircut when I was in kindergarten. He cut my hair short and shaved a small bald spot on the back of my head. My mother wouldn't let me go to school until the bald spot grew out again.

Of all my brothers and sisters (six in all), I am the only transplant to Athens, Ohio. I was born in Newark, Ohio, and have lived all around Southeastern Ohio. However, I moved to Athens to go to Ohio University and have never left.

At Ohio U, I never could make up my mind whether to major in English or Philosophy, so I got a bachelor's degree with a double major in both areas, then I added a Master of Arts degree in English and a Master of Arts degree in Philosophy. Yes, I have my MAMA degree.

Currently, and for a long time to come (I eat fruits and veggies), I am spending my retirement writing books such as *Nadia Comaneci: Perfect 10*, *The Funniest People in Comedy*, *Homer's* Iliad: *A Retelling in Prose*, and *William Shakespeare's* Hamlet: *A Retelling in Prose*.

By the way, my sister Brenda Kennedy writes romances such as *A New Beginning* and *Shattered Dreams*.

APPENDIX B: SOME BOOKS BY DAVID BRUCE

Retellings of a Classic Work of Literature

Arden of Faversham: *A Retelling*

Ben Jonson's The Alchemist: *A Retelling*

Ben Jonson's The Arraignment, or Poetaster: *A Retelling*

Ben Jonson's Bartholomew Fair: *A Retelling*

Ben Jonson's The Case is Altered: *A Retelling*

Ben Jonson's Catiline's Conspiracy: *A Retelling*

Ben Jonson's The Devil is an Ass: *A Retelling*

Ben Jonson's Epicene: *A Retelling*

Ben Jonson's Every Man in His Humor: *A Retelling*

Ben Jonson's Every Man Out of His Humor: *A Retelling*

Ben Jonson's The Fountain of Self-Love, or Cynthia's Revels: *A Retelling*

Ben Jonson's The Magnetic Lady, or Humors Reconciled: *A Retelling*

Ben Jonson's The New Inn, or The Light Heart: *A Retelling*

Ben Jonson's Sejanus' Fall: *A Retelling*

Ben Jonson's The Staple of News: *A Retelling*

Ben Jonson's A Tale of a Tub: *A Retelling*

Ben Jonson's Volpone, or the Fox: *A Retelling*

Christopher Marlowe's Complete Plays: Retellings

Christopher Marlowe's Dido, Queen of Carthage: *A Retelling*

Christopher Marlowe's Doctor Faustus: *Retellings of the 1604 A-Text and of the 1616 B-Text*

Christopher Marlowe's Edward II: *A Retelling*

Christopher Marlowe's The Massacre at Paris: *A Retelling*

Christopher Marlowe's The Rich Jew of Malta: *A Retelling*

Christopher Marlowe's Tamburlaine, Parts 1 and 2: *Retellings*

Dante's Divine Comedy: *A Retelling in Prose*

Dante's Inferno: *A Retelling in Prose*

Dante's Purgatory: *A Retelling in Prose*

Dante's Paradise: *A Retelling in Prose*

The Famous Victories of Henry V: *A Retelling*

From the Iliad to the Odyssey: *A Retelling in Prose of Quintus of Smyrna's Posthomerica*

George Chapman, Ben Jonson, and John Marston's Eastward Ho! *A Retelling*

George Peele's The Arraignment of Paris: *A Retelling*

George Peele's The Battle of Alcazar: *A Retelling*

George Peele's David and Bathsheba, and the Tragedy of Absalom: *A Retelling*

George Peele's Edward I: *A Retelling*

George Peele's The Old Wives' Tale: *A Retelling*

George-a-Greene: *A Retelling*

The History of King Leir: *A Retelling*

Homer's Iliad: *A Retelling in Prose*

Homer's Odyssey: *A Retelling in Prose*

J.W. Gent.'s The Valiant Scot: *A Retelling*

Jason and the Argonauts: A Retelling in Prose of Apollonius of Rhodes' Argonautica

John Ford: Eight Plays Translated into Modern English

John Ford's The Broken Heart: *A Retelling*

John Ford's The Fancies, Chaste and Noble: *A Retelling*

John Ford's The Lady's Trial: *A Retelling*

John Ford's The Lover's Melancholy: *A Retelling*

John Ford's Love's Sacrifice: *A Retelling*

John Ford's Perkin Warbeck: *A Retelling*

John Ford's The Queen: *A Retelling*

John Ford's 'Tis Pity She's a Whore: *A Retelling*

John Lyly's Campaspe: *A Retelling*

John Lyly's Endymion, The Man in the Moon: *A Retelling*

John Lyly's Galatea: *A Retelling*

John Lyly's Love's Metamorphosis: *A Retelling*

John Lyly's Midas: *A Retelling*

John Lyly's Mother Bombie: *A Retelling*

John Lyly's Sappho and Phao: *A Retelling*

John Lyly's The Woman in the Moon: *A Retelling*

John Webster's The White Devil: *A Retelling*

King Edward III: *A Retelling*

Mankind: *A Medieval Morality Play* (A Retelling)

Margaret Cavendish's The Unnatural Tragedy: *A Retelling*

The Merry Devil of Edmonton: *A Retelling*

The Summoning of Everyman: *A Medieval Morality Play* (A Retelling)

Robert Greene's Friar Bacon and Friar Bungay: *A Retelling*

The Taming of a Shrew: *A Retelling*

Tarlton's Jests: A Retelling

Thomas Middleton's A Chaste Maid in Cheapside: *A Retelling*

Thomas Middleton's Women Beware Women: *A Retelling*

Thomas Middleton and Thomas Dekker's The Roaring Girl: *A Retelling*
Thomas Middleton and William Rowley's The Changeling: *A Retelling*
The Trojan War and Its Aftermath: Four Ancient Epic Poems
Virgil's Aeneid: *A Retelling in Prose*
William Shakespeare's 5 Late Romances: Retellings in Prose
William Shakespeare's 10 Histories: Retellings in Prose
William Shakespeare's 11 Tragedies: Retellings in Prose
William Shakespeare's 12 Comedies: Retellings in Prose
William Shakespeare's 38 Plays: Retellings in Prose
William Shakespeare's 1 Henry IV, aka Henry IV, Part 1: A Retelling in Prose
William Shakespeare's 2 Henry IV, aka Henry IV, Part 2: A Retelling in Prose
William Shakespeare's 1 Henry VI, aka Henry VI, Part 1: A Retelling in Prose
William Shakespeare's 2 Henry VI, aka Henry VI, Part 2: A Retelling in Prose
William Shakespeare's 3 Henry VI, aka Henry VI, Part 3: A Retelling in Prose
William Shakespeare's All's Well that Ends Well: *A Retelling in Prose*
William Shakespeare's Antony and Cleopatra: *A Retelling in Prose*
William Shakespeare's As You Like It: *A Retelling in Prose*
William Shakespeare's The Comedy of Errors: *A Retelling in Prose*
William Shakespeare's Coriolanus: *A Retelling in Prose*
William Shakespeare's Cymbeline: *A Retelling in Prose*
William Shakespeare's Hamlet: *A Retelling in Prose*
William Shakespeare's Henry V: *A Retelling in Prose*
William Shakespeare's Henry VIII: *A Retelling in Prose*
William Shakespeare's Julius Caesar: *A Retelling in Prose*
William Shakespeare's King John: *A Retelling in Prose*
William Shakespeare's King Lear: *A Retelling in Prose*
William Shakespeare's Love's Labor's Lost: *A Retelling in Prose*
William Shakespeare's Macbeth: *A Retelling in Prose*
William Shakespeare's Measure for Measure: *A Retelling in Prose*
William Shakespeare's The Merchant of Venice: *A Retelling in Prose*
William Shakespeare's The Merry Wives of Windsor: *A Retelling in Prose*
William Shakespeare's A Midsummer Night's Dream: *A Retelling in Prose*
William Shakespeare's Much Ado About Nothing: *A Retelling in Prose*
William Shakespeare's Othello: *A Retelling in Prose*
William Shakespeare's Pericles, Prince of Tyre: *A Retelling in Prose*
William Shakespeare's Richard II: *A Retelling in Prose*
William Shakespeare's Richard III: *A Retelling in Prose*
William Shakespeare's Romeo and Juliet: *A Retelling in Prose*
William Shakespeare's The Taming of the Shrew: *A Retelling in Prose*

www.ingramcontent.com/pod-product-compliance
Lightning Source LLC
Chambersburg PA
CBHW031124160726
47989CB00016B/1068